T0095696

WE CAN'T ALL BE GEMS, ERASMUS VERMOUTH, SERIAL KILLER & ARTISTE

WE CAN'T ALL BE GEMS, ERASMUS VERMOUTH, SERIAL KILLER & ARTISTE

Two Novellas

CAROL ANN

We can't all be Gems, Erasmus Vermouth, serial killer & artiste
Two Novellas

iUniverse books may be ordered through booksellers or by contacting:

iUniverse
1663 Liberty Drive
Bloomington, IN 47403
www.iuniverse.com
1-800-Authors (1-800-288-4677)

Because of the dynamic nature of the Internet, any web addresses or links contained in this book may have changed since publication and may no longer be valid. The views expressed in this work are solely those of the author and do not necessarily reflect the views of the publisher, and the publisher hereby disclaims any responsibility for them.

Any people depicted in stock imagery provided by Thinkstock are models, and such images are being used for illustrative purposes only. Certain stock imagery © Thinkstock.

ISBN: 978-1-4917-9086-1 (sc)
ISBN: 978-1-4917-9087-8 (e)

Print information available on the last page.

iUniverse rev. date: 03/09/2016

Argument for Argument's Sake

"So you say you wish I were dead. I kinda' got that idea too. But then I find I cannot stand not to see your bilious, pimply face every day. I damn sure won't go near the stairwell when you're around, and I'll be damned if I'll eat the damned omelet you're shoving at me. Oh, yeah, 'Eat, Eat, you're breaking my heart.' Quit with the Jewish mother bullshit."

"Remember that scene in "Whatever Happened to Baby Jane?" with Joan Crawford in the wheelchair? And Joan said to Bettye's character, 'You wouldn't treat me this way if I weren't in a wheelchair.' And Bettye Davis says, 'But you are.' That's how I think things are going between you and me. You're a snotty bitch, Margie, and the first thing on Monday morning I'm cutting you out of the will. Oh, and you just had to say 50% of nothing is nothing. You just had to go for the jugular, Margie."

"Oh, yeah, I'm the lucky one. I have you to look after me. Yeah, real lucky. You lay on the couch all day watching talk shows, guzzling beer after beer and eating anchovy pizza. And then I have to wipe the vomit off your chin when you pass off. I'd kick your damn ass if I weren't crippled! Oh, and now you say I'm the reason you drink. When I was okay you still drank. At that time it was because your dad kind of came onto you a few times and you desisted but never told on him. Incest is all relative, dear. You're a sight for sore eyes, Margie. You look like a beached manatee in bra and panties. Your flesh is all mottled and gray looking. Why don't you go out once in a while? Oh, because you've got to look out for me. Well, that's goddamn touching, Margie. And Bullshit. You're clinically depressed is what you are."

"I don't like that manic gleam in your eyes. If you offed me they'd figure out it was you, and throw you in the slammer. No, I do not have enemies, you silly bitch, I was an IT man. Just think of eating all that lesbian pussy. Well, on the other hand you might like it. Oh, you say you would like that. Well, that could be the crux of the matter. But on the other hand, I can see why you wouldn't desire me sexually. Nobody likes a plate of limp noodles and the colostomy bag can't be a real turn on. I'm a reasonable man. I understand hardship. You say there never was a hard ship."

"Oh, you're witty when you want to be. I gotta' give you credit. You tell the best dirty jokes of all time. Yes, I know there are no Jews in jail: they eat lox (locks). That was funny, the first time, dear. You need some new material. Oh, Yeah, you say just looking at me would do the trick. A kinder woman I have never known. Not. What do you say it is. Alzheimer's or alcohol poisoning? Let's flip for it, heads is Alzheimer's. Tails, you're a hopeless drunk. What the fuck."

"So, now it's time for the Farmer's daughter jokes. Margie, you're a card. Could you please re-adjust your underwear. You're showing everything and it's turning my stomach. You know, Margie, you got spunk and I like that in a woman."

"Yes, Dear, I love you too. Want a stick of Juicy Fruit or Wrigley's Spearmint, Doll?"

What a Piece of Work is Man

"So Margie, you ask why I got myself in this fix? With this broken leg and concussion? No, Doll, It wasn't the mafia. Yes, Dear, I know they'd kill me if they knew me. But ii wasn't that. What can I say, last Tuesday three weeks ago, there was just a beautiful wind and the sun all ghastly bright, and the viridian green trees all dancing in the air and I was at the top of McGudger Hill. You see Barbara Cartland doesn't use words like viridian and you'd know that if you ever read anything else. I digress. I got to lookin' at the skate boarders, and I thought why don't I just go up the hill, then glide down the middle of the road and feel the breeze in my hair and there were no cars on either side. It was just perfect. I was wind surfing. What the Fuck. Well, I ran straight into this guys fancy red Lamborghini. I dented the trunk and the wheelchair just sort of went through the windshield, and I kinda just slid off the trunk and went unconscious but before I blacked out I hear him say, 'Jesus, it's raining paraplegics.'"

When I came to they told me I had a concussion and a broken left leg. I piped up and said, "Does this mean I'll never walk again?" Like in the old Black and white movies. "Sir, said the head honcho, "You have multiple sclerosis: you will never walk again you know that." I said, "My, my aren't we the rainer on parades," and spit up some blood. He replied, "Sir, I don't think this is the opportune time to joke around, you tried to kill yourself." I told him that was not my intent AT ALL and fuck him if he didn't believe me.

I informed the pissed off rich yuppie that yes, I had insurance but no, it would not cover this, and I told him I'd pay for his car repairs, and my hospital bills. The shrink stepped in and told me they were all concerned that I might try again to off myself and didn't I think a nice rest in the looney bin would be advisable after I healed physically. This was too funny and I broke into cackles again.

I said, "Dr. Nutmeg, or whatever your name is, I was just trying to have a good time. I was in no way trying to kill myself and it was very good until right at the end. Why would I try to kill myself when I've got so much to live for. All this." Sweeping my arm around to indicate the room. And here's the kicker, Margie. I said, "Why are you all so excited to keep me alive, just so I can die a slow agonizing death. You're real humanitarians." I gotta love it, Marge, for real.

"So, Marge, suffice it to say they put me in the farm of funny for two weeks. I would have called but what the fuck, I didn't want to worry you. I'm sorry, Doll. Kiss me on the lips and close your legs, there's a hole in the crotch and right now I don't want to look at your pussy if it's all the same to you."

"Those people at the Farm of Funny were so glad to see me go it was pathetic. I warned the Doc not to put me in as I would just fuck over their minds. Shit I had them all convinced that the staff were Santeria Witch Doctors and poisoning all of their meds. The staff was mostly black so they didn't need much convincing Also I used to dump out the contents of my colostomy bag on the floor and say, Oh, lookie I'm mentally ill and can't help myself. Those nurses really hated me.

"Marge, you should know that I'm loaded and that worked for Sun Oil in the IT department for thirty years before I got MS. I was never a file clerk. I'm not really poor. Now I know you're mad but try and control yourself. There's lots of people around in the building, Dear. You don't want witnesses to my murder." Then I really cracked up. This was a funny thing. It hurt me to laugh but I went on a laugh rampage.

Then Marge inquired why we lived in a shitty apartment with linoleum floors and dropped ceiling that faced a sewage plant and she was really hot. I could see the wheels turning in her little bottle red head.

"Darling, I said, "You little monster, I can see the wheels turning. Hey, hey Lizzie Borden, gave her mother forty whacks and when she was done gave her father forty-one." Marge expressed the notion that she did not think any of this was funny. Not a bit. I went on in this psychological vein.

"You're a psycho, hon. I knew it when I married you. You were the hottest tail I ever had. I envisioned great things. Like being a character in a Henry Miller book. You know, living on the edge. Sex, booze, and alcohol and cigarettes. You did not disappoint. Why would I marry a Brady Bunch mother. Now I can see you're really pissed. If it's any consolation I really pissed off the shrink, too. He even harrumphed at one point and I loved the shit out of that. It was like a Ronald Coleman movie where someone said something raunchy. Next I asked the nurse to see her twat 'because I was a dying man.' Oh, so funny."

"So, Doll watcha think? Let's go to Aruba and stay drunk the whole time. I'll even pay one of the big black studs to fuck if you're feeling neglected. The sky is the limit, Hon. Get off that damn couch, quit pigging out and stop trying to get cirrhosis. Live your life, Doll, and quit trying to die."

She said, "Ralphie. I do know some things. What a Piece of Work is Man. That's you, Ralphie," and she kissed me on the lips and put a hand on my limp cock.

Death is Some Scary Shit

"You know what, Margie. I think we both look great for our age in our own way. I know you're somewhat obese now and feel crestfallen, on the whole. But, lookit, girl, it's all proportional. You still got that tiny waist with giant tits and ass. You look like a Barby Doll who went off her diet. You're kind of like the Gaston Le Chaise sculpture of his old lady. And I still look like Rock Hudson before he got sick."

"Yeah, baby, it's not an empty compliment: I don't bull shit. You've got to know that. You look wonderful, you great, big, beautiful doll! That red hair makes you look like an Irish gun moll. You don't look American: you look European, exotic. Like a Fellini woman. The tobacconist out of Amarcord who whips out those great big beautiful tits. I'm a fuckin' lucky man, all things considered."

"You know when you get out of detox, we can take a long vacation to Aruba, or even Europe, if you want. Why should I hoard my wealth. Make hay while the sun's still shining. Carpe Diem, buttercup. Want to know what it means, Tempis Fugit. That's what it means. Okay, all right, I'm a college boy, white trash, yuppie whore. You're pissed I used big words. Babe, I aint about dumbing it down for you or anyone else. Come up to me: I won't step down for you. You could do with a little less Maury Povich and Jerry Springer, and that other shit you watch. Broaden your horizons like you broadened your ass. Now, don't pout because you look like an angry Persian cat. Quit saying, it's real life: they're actors or they round up all the mental defectives and put them in one place at one time. Come on, I think they're like the Snopes family

6

out of the sociology texts. They were this Appalachian family who were all screwing each other. Anyhoo, I'm sorry for being such a miser all this time. Fifteen goddamn years is a long time to have one's head up one's ass, n'est pas? Why'd you stick with me honey? It can't have been love: we fought like cats and dogs then went and screwed our brains out afterward. It was not my finest hour: I was such a condescending bastard. Forgive me, doll, I promise to treat you better now that I know you won't dispatch me."

She dimpled up in a pert smile and said, "When did I promise that". And then she practically busted a gut laughing. I laughed too, as I have a gallows sense of humor.

"I have a whole better attitude. And since I kept back the principle and didn't invest in stocks like everybody else, I am a rich man. And they are all out looking for jobs in theirs forties and fifties, and putting up for sale signs on their front lawns. To put it bluntly when I kick the bucket, you will be a fabulously wealthy woman. I've already set up the trust. I ask one thing that you go to college and get an English degree. I know, I know, I am a controlling bastard, but I want more for you in your life than TV and trashy porn movies, which, I admit I watched with you. I didn't try to help you or give you anything really valuable, like the gift of a mind. Now I'm going to do right by you and stand by you through all your travails only I won't actually be standing. A little witticism for you. Yeah, I know I joke too much. But it's like in the movie, The Sound of Music, 'a spoon full of sugar makes the medicine go down.' You'll live high on the hog. Papa done made enough money to bail out America. But, I'm not that selfless, and besides charity begins at home. But we'll make out a budget for you before I go!"

I started laughing and couldn't stop. Euphemisms always crack me up. He's in a better place now. He looks so peaceful with that smile. He never hurt a soul. He went in his sleep, the lucky bastard. The last is the funniest. Being dead is not analogous to "being lucky." Au contraire. Marge just looked at me in her cute, "you're out of your mind way." But I did not explain. She's used to me bursting out in laughter for no discernible reason.

At any rate, I planned to buy Marge a big, sumptuous house while she was away in rehab. I told her to cheer up, that she wouldn't have to come back to the shithole apartment, and I said, "Cheer up, doll, rehab won't kill you. Some of the best people on earth were alcoholics.

Betty Ford, for one. Ernest Hemingway, Alexander the Great, Drew Barrymore and my favorite female singer, Janis Joplin. Piece of My Heart, oh, yeah. I tell you better not backslide when you come back or I'll kick your pretty dimpled ass out the door and divorce you and you can go back to making your living studying ceilings. I'm not bullshitting you, Margie. You say you're scared. Well, babe, that's a given. Life is scary. Death is even more scary. What the Fuck, Living well is the Best Revenge. I was one stingy motherfucker. They say the truth will set you free. What a crock. More often it enslaves you. We are going to live like Scott Fitzgerald and Zelda only without the boozing and without mooching off rich patrons. No more nasty scraps of life. I will be bountiful. My accident really woke me up. Oh yeah, I wrote a poem for you since this is you last night of drinking on this earth. You deserve a send off. I hope you like it because I recorded it. I can't use my writing hand anymore but his you already know this. So crack open a cool one and get drunk as you want. This is your time, Babe."

DT'S, IF YOU PLEASE

DT's if you please. DT's if you please.
Reminiscent of a Boschian hell in 3D.
Go crawl up the giant egg, it wouldn't hurt.
On my God, you're such a flirt.
Yet your condition should cause some contrition.
This is no time to be a lady's man
Stand up if you can. Stand up if you can.
Rolling around on the floor: this is what I don't adore.
Little nude Marilyns doing the shimmy. Santa
Claus coming down the chimney.
Evil, green lizards gyrating to a Hendrix tune. Take
a bite of the cheddar that is the moon.
Roaches swarm like a Biblical plague. You
may as well go jump in a lake.
Liz Taylor lounging on your couch. Be a gentleman not a louse.
Dancing strawberries with fish net hose. Fish
heads staring up between your toes.
Snakes with lipstick on fucking themselves.
Wishing you could join a colony of elves.

There's a severed hand floating in your glass:
You don't know if this is the future or the past.
The maw of hell has opened for you and
no, you may not have a screw.

"That' it, Doll. I'm a fucking writer. How can I be whiter. It's no crime to rhyme."

You say only psychos rhyme. You'd be right about that.

It's Not Supposed To Be Fun

"Hell, Margie, you're in Rehab and it's not supposed to be fun. Get a Kleenex, for heaven's and wipe the vomit off your chin. Margie you look like hell, one of those Bettye Davis prison movies, where she comes up to the jail bars and says, "I want to live!" Doll, I told you I'd get by here every damn day and I do not disappoint. Oh, you say just kill you and put you out of your misery and there's a giant squid on the ceiling. Well, the killing part, I've thought on. Just put some rat pellets in your bran flakes and who'd be the wiser. As for the squid, that part is real. Psych! The killing part was a real heartfelt emotion.

No, I don't feel that way, now. Anyhoo, how would I do it? I can't use my hands part of the time. I couldn't pull it off. Oh, hon, the worst part is behind you. Where's that fighting Irish spirit of yours. Oh, we don't like our roommate do we. A big black lezzie who wants us to lick her pussy. Like the commercial says, "Just say no. Look on the bright side, if you weren't so beautiful she wouldn't be after you. Homely people don't get called on to suck pussy. You should count your blessings. I didn't mean it when I called you a beached manatee. I'm sorry, sometimes I'm a real SOB." I saw the roommate galumphing into the room, and I whispered to Margie, "Here comes Aunt Jemima,".

I can be very assertive and this is what I said, "Listen, miss, I don't appreciate you coming onto my wife. How'd you like me to brain you with this goddamned wheelchair? Laugh now, but how'd you like a concussion, or maybe I could just split your head open like a ripe cantaloupe. What do I have, I have MS, Miss. Ok lookey, Papa made a rhyme. You know I'm crippled and you're laughing your big black ass off. Oh, 'Go fuck myself,' you say. Would if I could. Now that is a very uncharitable notion Miss. What is your name, sweetheart? Oh, Sha Nay Nay. Well, aren't you the original one. Imagine a black person with the name of Sha Nay Nay. I scarcely noticed you were black."

"Now you're going to brain me with your flower pot. At one point in my life I was a criminal trial lawyer. Got out of it. Too stressful. But I know a shitload of people, somewhat nefarious. You can well imagine, some disagreeable, horrible cocksuckers and your homeboys, or corner boys, as I like to call them, are just not up to my level. Everything Is just a matter of degree. This place give me the creeps, the padded cells, the overhead fluorescent lights, the starchiness of their white uniforms with the hard candy smiles plastered on their faces. How'd you like to do an extended stay just to make sure they don't release you too soon. I can arrange that, doll."

"I just had an awful inclination: to comment on your appearance. You need Jenny Craig desperately. God, woman are your tits on a pulley system to make 'em pop out like this. Do men make little Smiley faces on the flesh while making love. I'm guessing you're Bi. Could he even get to your luscious cunt."

"Oh, I'm a motherfucker, right? Well on the whole it seems like a good idea. You should see my mom. Really hot. I'd be willing. Don't think I haven't thought of it: my mom's a knockout."

"Now, you say that's just nasty and perverted. Sure it is: All the very things that are make the best things in life. That's why I look out for my Margie. She got the hottest tail this side of the Rio Grande. She was a pole dancer when I met her. I like my women a little on the trashy side. Am I disturbing you, Doll. There's more than one way to skin a cat. I'm a crazy motherfucker: I'm clean out of my head."

And if you don't leave Margie alone you shall meet some of my friends from my lawyering days. Crazy mother fuckers, all of them and they' put a straight edge right up where the moon don't shine." I put on my angry pissed off face and further said, "It is also your duty to keep the other dykes off her ass."

"You is crazy, Mistah, I just tries it because sometimes 'No' they really means yes. Ya' know. "I bet you're a real blast at traffic lights is all I can say. Doll, 'no' means no and you leave her the fuck alone and protect her while she's here."

"Okay Okay. Ya aint have to get offensive wid' me., Mistah'", she said.

"Now, I see you're a nice young lady. You may go now that we've had our little fireside chat," I said."

Then Marge made a quick pilgrimage to the bathroom and I could her gagging and vomiting. It was not her finest hour. She came out all drained and shaky and walked into my arms such as I was.

"Ralphie, you're in a class by yourself. What a Piece of Work Is Man. Willy S."

"That's a given baby," I replied.

Therapy

I got give Margie credit for putting up with the therapy. The old gal's got some stamina. My prickly little doll can be quite witty though she doesn't have a college degree. She called it "Tit for Tat" since there were so many low cut tee shirts with "Foxy Bitch, Baby Doll, and Queen Bitch" on their shirts. Actually if you have to say you're a Queen Bitch you're usually a wimp. Bitches always hide that kind of information until you've got your pants down, then they bring out the whips and heavy leather. I shit you not. She called them "Untermenchen" which is German for low life. I feed her bits of culture which she gobbles up like a hungry harpy. They say you can lead a whore to culture but you can't make her think. That's not the case with my Badass Doll. She absorbs culture like a fuckin' sponge. Now there's a facsimile of her early whoredom which crops up every now and then but, hey, nobody's perfect. She really has a good mind and I know she'll do fabulously in college. In case you forgot, getting an English degree is a requirement for her to collect on this humongous trust fund I set up for her. She'll live like a fuckin' queen (no, not that kind of queen). You know I intuit a lot about people and sometimes understand them better than they understand themselves. I knew under all that trash she was a fine person, though I learned it a little late. Fifteen years is a bit late in the game but better now than never. I was a first class bastard and she only came at me once with a knife. Right there that proves she's a good woman. Any other woman would have killed me, the running around on her, the making her beg for money for little things like make-up, and clothes. Made her buy all her clothes from WalMart and I was a fuckin'

millionaire. I always, took her to the buffet once a week so I wasn't a total bastard, or was I? Hmm. I just had this fear that she'd kill me and run off with the cabana boy but God bless her she never cheated, took her marriage vows very seriously. I always fear people will only like me for the money. So I really poor mouthed her for fifteen years and then I started to get sick. And still she didn't leave. To be a former whore Margie's very straight like Hester Prynne of the Scarlet Letter. She was so depressed and I made her an alcoholic. Mea Culpa. I criticized her, belittled her and was insanely jealous, thinking she was always carrying on behind my back. Yep, she was a victim and always felt ashamed of herself and took my words to heart. I tell ya getting sick makes a man take stock of himself. And I found Ol' Ralphie quite lacking. That was when I knew I had to help her and treat her right. Hence the therapy. I don't give a shit whether she wanted me dead. A person can only take so much abuse. I had it coming. I'm going to get us a big fuckin' house on the Mainline where the rich cavort. And she'll have plenty of company in the whoredom thing. Lots of hookers marry rich men. I got a full nine inches and was not loath to use it and she fucked like all hell. We had a beautiful sex life. She never said "no" morning or night time. We fucked like a pair of jack rabbits.

Margie doesn't like the women because they are stupid, and low class. Margie was a Victoria Secret Whore not a Fredericks type succubus. Or Suck Your Bus. I had to do that. I think I'm funny even if no one else does. She was smart enough to know I'd never hit her and that she could argue with me and not end up with a black eye. These women in their skin tight jeans, and slogan tee shirts and tennis shoes and flip flops did not do much for her. And they had the kind of brassy gold earrings with their names on it. Like they wanted people to say, "There's goes Tamika, she walketh on water." Margie wore Calvin Klein skirts and pants and high stilettos from Macys. She saved enough from the budget to once in a while get a nice piece of clothing or jewelry. She really could pinch a penny. Then she began to really be an alcoholic and wore tees and just her undies all day and disappeared into the Maury show or Jerry Springer show. The moving TV screen became her reality. I'm not even sure she saw the crass posturing of the contestants. I think she just lived in her poor painful head.

Oh, yeah, back to the therapy chicks it was the same old story. Physically abusive husbands and reams of children to make it almost impossible to get away. None of them were smart enough to stop popping the babies out of their cunts like chickens laying eggs. And because Marge looked like she was in better shape they ostracized and victimized her. And they told her she had a rich husband and no real problems. So one day she stood up and offered to kick all their asses and no knives allowed. "Listen," she said. "You bitches do have a way out. Leave the bastards, move into a shelter, take your kids with you and get an education to support them. Or stay until he finally kills you. Which is the best thing that could happen to you. I listened to you say these men love you and that the beatings were caused by something you did. Stay, get killed, have more babies, I could give a shit. But don't tell me my story: my husband, whom I love very much, is dying and that won't change. So, go on, you stupid cows and believe they love you. Oh, yes, Darlings, let them kill you. I can't stand the sight of you and don't think I won't kick your asses if you hassle me anymore!"

There was a stony silence and the silly ass, Meg Ryan look-alike social worker, "thanked her for sharing." And this really irritated Margie. She told this woman, "Why do you have this job, bitch. Do you just like the company of losers or is the salary generous. I suspect the latter. They wouldn't have the sense to get in a life boat if it were the Titanic. And you don't have any sense either to have a job like this. Just like sweeping up the detritus."

After that, the woman called security and they escorted Marge to a padded cell. As she was being forcefully ejected, "You think this alters the reality of what I said? Truth hurts doesn't it? See, you in Hell, bitches" And she wrote rather crude poetry in there. Poems' like "You're a cunt licker/ Mommy's little Yorky." "I love you/ Poke me in the ass." She did this to incense the social worker to whom she gave them, apologizing for her "former bad attitude".

After that they left her on her own and she sat in stony silence at the "group meetings"

I fucking love this woman and I am going to give her heaven and hell, and all that goes in between. She's My Special Angel. You know the song.

Just Us Little Chickens

How weird is this. I got Margie a small mansion on the mainline with a porch and Ionic columns with real marble floors and seraphs painted on the high ceilings. Makes you think Michelangelo was here. Just us little chickens in an eight room, three story, three bathroom palace. There's even a terrazzo tiled floor like in olden times with the original refurbished cabinets in the kitchen. Place dates back to the 1900's. Maybe one of the heroine's out of Louisa May Alcott's Little Woman lived here. I'd like to think it was Jo. I could tell you what it cost but what the hey? I don't feel like it. But I will volunteer the information that I'm rich as Croesus. I'd bend over and kiss my own ass if I could. Bon Chance.

Marge was overcome with emotion like when Peckie the canary died. She fell into my arms like a stray bolt of yellow silk. I thought she'd bawl her head off but fortunately it stayed intact. Thank God for small favors. I just am not into headless dames. It's amazing ladies still go for me, (one even asked me if I was intact "down there"). I licked the tip of my nose with my serpentine tongue in a way of explaining and she laughed and kissed me on the cheek. I do like sex even though I no longer directly benefit from it. Love the smell of woman under my nose and I love to drive Marge to ecstasy.

Sometimes I get ticked off at God. Sadistic motherfucker. But I end up kissing his celestial ass as I'm dying to get into heaven. A little witticism for you. I tell you when Margie got out of Rehab she looked like a fuckin' movie star. Isn't it funny how all the ugly people hang together. I guess water seeks its own level as they say. She lost forty pounds and tightened up her former blubber. Amazing for a coupla' months! Now Margie drinks V-8 juice all day long with Tabasco in it. Says it reminds her of Bloody Marys. After she gets more stable we'll depart for Aruba and then Paris and London and Italy. Fuck the English. Never met one I liked, those slick bastards. What the hey! She says she wanted to try English cuisine and I said cuisine is not what they have.

Anyhoo, I'm a little scared of Hell as I saw Bosch's Garden of Earthly Delights. I screwed a shit load of people financially and spiritually when I was a criminal defendant lawyer. Guilty as Heidnick and Bernie Maddoc all around. Still I got them off. I'm not proud of myself for that. All and all I went from the "screwer" to "the royally screwed". And I had the love of a good woman and took her for granted. Sure Margie's a psycho. Silly shit like the neighbors stealing all our close pins, or I'm fucking the old, toothless Spanish maid. People really like her though she's got a condition. Margie's the most generous person I know. Give you the shirt off her back then bitch slap you on the cheeks with her voluminous tits. She's like that. Unpredictable, but ever so sweet. Never bitched me out for being so stingy. What a fucker I was, and she loved me with all her heart and never ever cheated. Can't say that for me, sorry. There's got to be some sort of poetic justice in this.

I guess I love Marge more than anyone ever even myself but I'm not a self hating bastard. If I were, I could not love anyone and that's a real true thing in life. No, my self esteem is fine, thank you very much. I'm a good looking bastard. When we get to Aruba I'm going to hire a big, black stud with a stainless steel dick. Fuck her from sun up to sun down or vice versa. Like I used to do.

Listen, in life, you got to be like Dame Largesse. She was a medieval character, who rode around the peasant countryside freely giving wine, cheese, bread to the starving masses. She was their Martha Stewart. Fuckit! Live Large, you bastards.

Hobnobbing with the Hogoblins

Lately, while Marge recuperates I've been sneaking out to the after hours bars to feed my sense of noir. While Little Miz Moffit sleeps. Oh, she'd be pissed it she knew. I get to meet the real raptors: they sit on their stools like vultures sitting on a carcass. The really depressed, down on their luck losers.

I'm a handsome guy and even though I'm in a wheelchair I always attract antiquarian pussy. I can smell the rot on them, along with the rancid smell of spent lives rising in the air in paisleys of cigarette smoke. I collect their grievous stories like semi-precious stones. I am a handsome guy and a good listener. I don't reveal my own malaise, that my time on earth will be short. Hell, life's beautiful… and brutal.

Here's a typical story and I quote on ruddy, misshapen miss. "That bastard left me for an eighteen year old stripper. She didn't even have a smattering of education. I've got a Masters in Art History wind a minor in English literature." Like that contained some useful reference, I thought but did not say. "Education for education's sake is a crock if shit. It prepares you to be a waitress or to clean out toilets. I got a "hard" degree, one that trains you to actually work. I actually did real things in life, lawyering and then an IT degree. English majors, hear me. Tone up your midriff and marry well. Marrying well is the best revenge." Since unless you're a successful writer which will be unlikely. Everybody thinks they're brilliant when most times it's just well decorated bytes of misery. He done her wrong stories abound in romance fiction, then this ordinary chick trades up to this glorious, adoring hunk.

Like that's a real thing. I read romances and laugh my head off. I love it when the square jawed, irascible hunk realizes he must have this gray sparrow ordinary as mud. These babes I find in here are just too replete with misery and self loathing to attract a decent man. But I give them warmth and understanding. It doesn't cost anything to be kind. Why not try to help somebody. It's actually part of my strategy to get into Heaven, that is, if it exists.

Sartre may be right. Life is absurd. But this philosophy does not warm the cockles of the heart. I prefer, "Life is real: life is earnest," by whomever wrote it and the advice of Auntie Mame. "Life is a banquet and most poor bastards are starving."

I tell em. "Look you're still attractive. Don't ruin your looks and your waistline by drinking like a fish. Don't just live on the alimony. Don't be a spurned woman. Don't adopt that as a philosophy because you're better than that. Love and respect yourself: don't wallow in misery. Remember, what I say. Only the strong survive, and strength cannot be conveyed or given. It must be learned. Find yourself some girlfriends and quit looking for 'Mister Wonderful' to make it all better. Get a real education and a real job. You are not half of two but one of one. You are the master of yourself. You are complete within yourself."

They kiss me all over the face for that one. Nobody likes a wilted flower as it has putrescence, and that's a harsh reality. I don't tell them this. I do not wish to injure, only to encourage. I like helping people and this helps me. It really does. I help the men too, who are dying of the same malaise. Thinking life is a meaningless and painful experience. Thinking in life, God gave you a raw deal. Life is a beautiful, and brutal proposition. I call these little forays into the underworld my "missions of mercy".

I remember one time in the eighties when I was quite young and going to Dirty Franks Bar. This is from my early journals.

GOD

Never ever go to Dirty Franks Bar if you're tripping on window pane. That's real badass Acid in case you don't know. And yes, I learned the hard way. It all coalesced halfway through my fourth Rolling Rock, the Po' man's juice as "the brothers" are wont to say. Giant purple Bermuda onions with red fish net hose and high toeless stilettos were gyrating obscenely on top of the bar, I mean it was raunchy, low-down and gritty like bad porn. They were shedding their skins like burlesque strippers, their skins leaving a sticky mush on top of the bar. Then after they peeled out, a little witticism for you, they vanished into thin air. POOF! Then this Giant Eye with multiple octopus tentacles sat down next to me and said, "Hello, Ralphie, I'm God." He grinned like "Goofy Grape" showing he was gap toothed. And this kind of freaked me out as I was reading Chaucer's Canterbury Tales, The Wyfe of Bath specifically. See all things are connected like cigarettes and lime jello. I really am on to something. You get it, too, I can tell.

So much for the antics of youth. Oh, well. I lived it well.

MINOTAUR

The Old Gal and I are in Aruba now in a cottage apartment. Tres Luxurious, three rooms, kitchen stocked with fruits, steak, fish, chesses and vegetables and an entire liquor cabinet, which I had removed, and a sumptuous four poster bed complete with filmy canopy. And the brocade couch makes you feel like a pearl ensconced in velvet. Oh, Lord, am I happy. We spend our days going to the beach and drinking virgin Pina Coladas as waiters come down to the beach and inquire what we want.

Margie's kind of edgy without the liquor and having to deal with reality and all. But it happens to the best of us. But bless her heart, the Old Gal's staying straight aside from the occasional joint we share. I feel like a corn fed goose. I am grinning like a fox in the hen house. Happy as a one-eyed cat in a barrel full of fish heads. I like those southern sayings. I had a roommate from Alabama in college and he was a font of southern wisdom.

The sea is absolutely unforgettable, a kind of mixture of viridian green and indigo, and the smell of it is like talcum powder and pearls. The sand is startlingly white like it's been bleached and warm as a puppy's nose. The sky at night is pink, orange and purple brush strokes made by God. We go to the beach every day to watch the parade of pulchritude, as I call it. Do no fat, ugly people go on vacation here? Margie says, "You know we can't all be gems."

They must all live in the sewers with the rats. I get this horrid picture of a fat person biting into a rat's stomach and I grimace. Margie notices but says nothing. She knows I get these visual images of camels fucking or mermaids drowning pirates so she just doesn't ask anymore. Or if I were to start laughing out of the blue at nothing at all she knows not to ask. I got this image last Christmas of Santa's elves fucking Snow White, and had a real laugh riot. How would they reach her pussy. It still cracks me up. Then there was the day that I told her dandelion fluff resembles Dr. Einstein's hair. She said fine but not to go around telling people what was in my head. Good advice.

Margie and I are all oiled up in sun block SP-35. No sense in courting wrinkles. Stay young, die beautiful is my motto. Ugliness turns me off. I know it's shallow. So I'm a shallow motherfucker. I think ugliness is a breeding ground for envy and Machiavellian thoughts. But then there's Mother Therese. I can find no fault in her. There are exceptions to my rule. I'm still built with a six pack stomach and muscled arms and legs as I was a body builder when I was well. And Margie is curvy like a windy road going to hell.

Guys are really swarming all over her like bees in a fuckin' hive. Then she flashes that mega carat wedding ring I gave her and they dispense like scalded dogs. Oh, there are other girls, chic and hard bodied, but they prefer my Margie's lushness like a fifties movie star. I'm wearing a speedo and Margie is wearing a black studded bikini which leaves little to the imagination. I notice one of the men stubbornly remains and according to my plan, he's "The One". When Marge comes back I tell her to invite him over and Margie says I'm out of my fuckin' mind. I reply with Emily Dickenson's Poem, "Much Madness is Divinest Sense,".

When he gets to me, he says, "Ah, Dawg, I'm sorry I didn't know you were her husband. My bad. I really apologize. I kinda' lost my head. Your woman looks like she could tear into a steak. These other bitches look like they're lettuce eaters. She's just so bodacious." His black skin shined like burnished obsidian.

"Yes," I reply. "The Land of the Lotus Eaters. A little witticism for you. How much for today and all night?"

"Oh, I don't do freaky shit, mister. Besides I'm not a whore."

"I mean you and my wife," I said, "And I get to watch. And the name's Ralph."

"Oh, shit this is getting weird. I don't do weird, Ralph, or whatever your name is."

"Look, I'm crippled and I want my woman to enjoy herself. Do you have a good nine inches for her enjoyment? I will pay $1000, with $500 down."

"Can I see ID on both of you and search your cabin for weapons and don't try to get me to eat or drink anything," he says. "I got the nine inches, and positively no S&M. I'm Mohammed."

"Mohammed, what an original name for a black man. I thought you were going to say 'Mortimer'", I said

Margie pitched a fuss but I could see she had a hunger for this blue black, bulge in the pants, motherfucker. He was a huge guy in body as well. I said to Marge, "Methinks the Lady Doth Protests Too Much," and laughed my ass off. Marge was all over me with kisses and hugs and she called me the sweetest human being who ever lived.

After he assented, having checked us out, and finding no weapons, Cupid and his arrows descended. But not before I prepared the boudior with dozens of white roses and lighted candles with aromatic scents and put down the blinds, and locked the door. I also turned down the sheets and put two mints on the bed. You may as well try to keep up the humor.

He rubbed down her whole body with eucalyptus oil front and back, and when he got to her feet she began moaning as her feet are one of her erogenous zones. He began to kiss them and tongue her toes. Then she flipped over and opened her pink and white orchid for him to plunder with his turgid, purple cock. He had not lied, he was built like a bull. It all became pretty mythological to me. A young, innocent maiden ravaged by a minotaur amongst the sighing viridian grasses kissed by the cold silvery rays of a jealous moon. The whispering of the waves filled my ears and my eyes filled with tears of jealousy and love. And I wished I were a god, too. Oh, Margie, glowing hot like the embers of a fire. Oh, Margie, sweet orchid.

Like an Egyptian Slave Girl

I was up first in the morning and looked in on the sleeping two. And thought of Hank Williams singing "Cold, Cold Heart." The pain and the raspiness of Hank's voice held my heart in much the same way as a child hold's a butterfly in his hand. Mohammed with one arm draped over her tits, both sleeping in spoon fashion. No use crying over spilt semen I told myself. The Rape of the Sabine Woman. Uh huh.

I determined to order up a sumptuous breakfast, steaks, fish, muffins, large fruit bowl, various egg dishes, a pitcher of Mimosas and a pot of good Arabian coffee. Margie's "Prom" night, that's what it was. Her "Debutante" party. It was a feast worthy of Dame Largesse. I am no stingy little boy nor jilted husband. I was going to show my woman a good time for all the years of privation.

Mohammed, "The Minotaur" awoke with a start and quickly covered their nude bodies with a sheet with a telltale bulge beneath the sheet. I ignored his sheepish look, and asked if he enjoyed my wife.

"More, than any man could ask for," replied Mohammed with down cast eyes.

"Lookit, stop being so shamefaced, I invited you into my bed to fuck my wife. There's no shame here. Don't worry so, Mohammed, this isn't the part where I get out the shot gun and off both of you in lurid yellow journalism style. It's what you're thinking, isn't it?"

Mohammed let out a bray of laughter. "A black man not lynched for being with a white woman. Quelle sorpresse."

'You speak French?"

"And Italian, German, Chinese and my own tongue, Swahili," he said.

"Oh, you're a linguist. A cunning linguist, pun intended."

"I'm in my senior at U Penn. I'm thirty years old and got kind of a late start. Papa needed me and then he passed away and I decided I wanted more from life," he said.

"Hell, the way you're stacked, why don't you be an escort. A Richard Gere thing, Swahili Gigolo kind of thing?"

"No, thank you. This is not my scene. I shall be a translator for a Fortune 500 company and I shall have a fine wife, dark as the black hole from my home town. No offense to your lady. She is really supreme," he said.

"Oh, you don't have to tell me. Hot as the devil's chili pepper's. I could never get enough of her. She loves sex. Then I got sick."

"I'm sorry, man."

"Relax, I have fun all the time. A wheelchair can't define me. I'm livin' large. Just wait until I get this cast off. Gonna do the Handicapped Olympics."

"You're a helluva guy. I don't think I could be so generous. With my wife, that is."

"We're from Philly, too, the mainline. Drop by when the wolf is at your door sometime. Have another, go at it, so to speak," I said.

"Well, Ralph. I will and I don't think I ever met anyone like you. Suis generis," he said.

"Yeah, I get that a lot. Sometimes I hang out at anthills for inspiration just to see them carry something ten times larger than they are and what for to get squashed under someone's foot. And lookit the caterpillar turns into a butterfly. Don't worry about me, I'll make it. Then I'll die and go poof."

Ralph, you mean it doesn't depress you."

"No, Hell, no. I went through the "why me?" stage and then I looked at what a grasping, bitter, stingy cock sucker I'd been and said, 'Okay, God, you have a point.' If you don't worry about what's happening you won't worry about what's going to happen."

Mohammed said he worried about the economic climate and whether he would actually get a job.

I said, "Nothing's ever enough, Mohammed. You may as well know that now. Court Lady Luck, and never stiff anyone. Pray to whatever

God's there may be. Take this quote from A.E. Henley, 'Black is the night that falls upon me, Black as the pit from pole to pole. I thank whatever gods there may be for my unconquerable soul.' Say, would you like a robe, I keep staring at your dick and I think I might be gay." Then I busted out in laughter. Oh, life is way funny. I'm not kidding. "Want a blow job?" And I kept laughing. Sometimes, I crack myself up.

Mohammed let out a bray of laughter and took the robe and said, "You know there was this farmer and he had a lusty, beautiful daughter and a salesman came to the door, and she was nude.." And Mohammed just cracked up. "I think you Americans have a patent on the best jokes. I love that farmer's daughter stuff."

"I got one." I said, "There was this one really cheap hit man named Artie who did hits for a dollar because he was so bad at it. He followed this industrialist around for a month and every time he got a bead on him, someone stepped in front of him. Finally he got so disgusted he followed him into the Acme, and garroted him. There was one lady in the line to get fresh fish who saw him so he had to kill her, too. Then the fish man got all bug eyed and started to scream and Artie choked him, too. Not surprisingly, Artie got caught as he was not the brightest bulb in the package. Know what the headline read the next day? Artie chokes three for a dollar."

"That's the most stupid joke I have ever heard," replied Mohammed.

"Isn't it though. I love stupid things except for the politicians. Human vermin!"

"Ralph, do you say it's all luck in the serious sense?' he said

"Luck, effort, and humor. If you laugh at life, God likes you. He hates a sour puss." I said.

"Excuse me, what is sour puss. Do you mean oral sex?" Mohammed asked.

"No, it means a naysayer and a rainer on parades. A no joy boy."

"Oh, you mean the Ebenezer Scrooge, Dickens?" he said.

"Amen, brother. Say, you're a student why not come by alone, and have Christmas with us. Do you play chess. I was a Grand Master, once," I said.

"Oh, now, you want to play games with me?' he said and brayed.

"Sure, I do and then, need I say it, you could be one of Margie's gifts. Life is like a Rubix Cube, you can't quite solve it but you can come close if you're really good. And I'm really good. Shall we wake our sleeping princess. She kind of looks like a Botero only not as fat and round. And she's wearing an anklet, sexy as hell. Like an Egyptian slave girl."

Mohammed said that he read somewhere that anklets signified a wish to be strangled.

"Whoa, wait a minute, there, cowboy. That's way out in left field. Anklets indicate that she likes you to chew on her pinkies. It's called attention to the feet."

Margie yawned and stretched like a yellow tabby in the sun light.

"Do I smell steaks," she queried.

"Yes, you do, my love. We've been waiting for you to initiate our feast. We've got rare peppered porterhouse, salmon, tilapia, mushroom and gouda omelettes, and bran muffins, your favorite. While, I warm it up, in the meantime, hit the fruit bowl. And have a mimosa. Hell knows, we've been knocking 'em back.

You know I can't, Ralphie. I'll have coffee, with cream and sugar."

"Good Girl, always on her toes or her ass."

"Oh, Ralphie, you're pissed, aren't you?

"No, babe, I'm Shakespeare and I wrote this little passion play, and I'm King Lear and you're Cordelia, and I'm Hamlet, 'Mad but mad, North, Northwest.," and you're the "mad" Ophelia." I'm Every Man, and yes, I'm jealous as hell. But if you ever knew me at all, you'd know I don't hold grudges. That's for spoiled children."

"Oh. Ralphie, I love you so," she said and hugged me.

"Margie, I love you like midnight, soft black, velvet and the stars all twinkling like hell. You're my soft, warm pearl."

Money Doth Make Bitches of Us All

We stayed in Aruba until October and there were frequent forays with Mohammed and he genuinely liked us both quite a lot and we made plans for him to spend the Christmas season as a house guest. He was handsome, erudite, an all round decent human being and of course, I could afford his little forays into our lives and I know it was not just the money he came for. He was quite smitten with Margie and liked the hell out of me. It was truly a mutual admiration society, just a little skewed as I was always the silent watcher. Images of Margie coming floated through my head like misty ghosts and it made me more sexual. I began to have hard-ons and Margie was attentive enough to notice and do something about them. I felt a new vitality and like any doomed person, I began to hope. Hope can save you or break you. I was passionate and in love with the world, and Margie, too, more than ever.

We arrived in Paris on Halloween night. Everywhere sinister, grimacing pumpkins lined the walkways or peered from the windows. And I thought of our new arrangement, and I realized it was like Cyrano de Bergerac, a man hiding in the bushes whispering the odes of love to another man, who would take my place in her bed. Bittersweet, lush life and how the naked trees resembled knotted, arthritic old men's limbs and the moon was a sly fingernail clipping in the inky black sky of multitudes of rhinestone stars. It was very dark and it made the revelers in their costumes even more vivid. Shades of Mandarin orange, soft black velvet, greens and scarlets. I was reminded of E. A. Poe's poem, Masque of The Red Death, and I was in the thirteenth room, and I laugh at death. I've got a new corny joke for you. Why do people love the asylums? Because they're chock full of nuts.

The masks were incredible, falcon masks, peacock masks, and those evil looking jester masks on a stick. Paris is a holiday for the adults in Paris. Insane cackles of laughter like witches' laughter faded in and out of hearing range, and I can smell the death of fall leaves on the passageway. We stayed at the Hotel Secret de Paris at 2 Rue de Parme. We just liked the name and the red painted walls in the bedroom with a pastel pink coverlet on the beds. It was quite spacious as it is a suite and merciful heavens, it had a splendid liquor cabinet with hard liquors like Salignac, liquers like Kahlua and Crème de Menthe, and Cointreu, And a wide assortment of wines. If I die soon let it be in Paris in this room. We both like secrets and have no inclination to map one another's psyche. Some things belong in the dark and rain and are not made to be shared. Margie never pries nor studies me nor analyzes me. And the same for me.

And they placed a long stemmed white rose across the numerous pillows on our beds every time we went out. I tell you it was splendid. What was interesting s that they left the thorns on the roses as f to say," Life is both beautiful and also treacherous." Maybe I'm just dying to find hidden messages in life because I know I'm dying. Maybe that's it and maybe people just aren't as subtle as I think they are. They knocked on our door at ten in the morning with a complimentary breakfast, Arabica coffee, cream and honey, freshly squeezed orange juice, tomato juice, a crystal bowl of freshly cut fruit of strawberries, blueberries, bananas, melons, grapes and the like. And the most delicious chocolate and juniper croissants I have ever had. They gave us just enough and no more. I like that, a healthy animal is a slender animal. And you may quote me on that. In fact, quote everything I say: I'm just like Soloman. Oh yeah, I forgot, they changed flowers in our room every day when we went out, everything from chrysanthemums to tuberoses. It's not always the big things in life, you know. It's the little acts of kindness that warm the soul. The places we went I'll list and then tell you our favorites. The Louvre, Le Musee d'Orsay, the Eiffel Tower (at night, wowie), Le Jardin de Tuileries, Notre Dame Cathedral (took 100 years to build), le Arc de Triomphe, le Centre Georges Pompidou, Sacra Cour and Montmartre, Pere Lachaise Cemetery, and a boat tour on the Seine River.

Let me tell you Margie, looked stunning every day in her fresh bold colors of hot pink, orange, green, lavender for the day and at night, black cocktail dresses with diamond jewelry for dinner. She oft wore a red straw hat in homage to Renoir's Women in the Red Hat and this was not lost on the French who said we were definitely not "The Ugly Americans." I have to say my favorite was gliding down the Seine watching Paris slip by my eyes like a water color print. Margie's favorite was the Musee de' Orsay for wondrous Impressionistic paintings of Monet, Degas, and others. Oh, those water lilies and the faint pale skin of the dancers. Oh, beauty, the ointment for the soul. We loved Le Jardin de Tuileres, so fragrant and alive, flowers just bursting forth, impermanent and lovely. Like all men and women. A baby is born then spends its life in the shadow of death, never too far away. We both liked the Louvre and spent an entire day there, so vast was it. The old paintings of the Christ on the cross, his flesh so transparent as if we could see the life draining out of him. Dolorous brown eyes like you find on a dead deer. Very evocative and affecting. Ancient suits of armor, so small were the men and much shorter than the men of today. We went to see the Palace of Versailles built by Louis XIV, the "Sun King", the greatest Monarch to ever live and the most brilliant. He made it law that his nobles had to live in town and not on their estates making it impossible for them to wage war on Him. Their fates were translated into how well they appeased King Louis. Then He made his palace a work of Art, the grandest structure in all the world. Louis's main talent was in surrounding himself with brilliant people, like Jean Claude Colbert, Prime Minister and artists like Voltaire and Rabelais. He also spent heavily on war expansion of territories and works of art. The wars vanished leaving only beauty behind. History is nothing but a record of the pathology of war.

Margie and I decided to play a game. She dressed like a street whore with a bustier and colored crepe de Chine micro mini of a roseate color, and lots of turquoise eye shadow on her almond colored eyes and metallic looking purple lipstick and I bought a loud cheap chartreuse suit and some Gitanes, which are French cigarettes, and put them in an embossed silver case in my pocket. I don't usually smoke and this was for show and I also took five hundred dollars in twenties with me. I slicked my hair down with pomade, and Marge piled her auburn hair up in a crude French twist. We made our way into the belly of the whale, so to speak, an underground basement bar in the rough Monmartre area of Paris, aptly named "Bon Chance Cabaret". The door man blocked our entrance demanding to know who sent us, and off the top of my head, murmured in a low guttural voice, "Jules sent us". The door man embraced me and said, "Quelle Homme, I thought he had died."

"No, he's rather dangerously alive as you must realize," I said, and we made our serpentine way to the crowded area of the bar.

A fat blond Lady offered us chocolate cherries from a red cardboard heart and Margie took a few to show she was "simpatico" and not an outsider. She really took a shine to Margie and asked if she'd like to work for her as she was a well established Madame and always looking for "fresh meat". Margie answered her in French, which I do not speak, but from the look on the Madame's face, I saw a mixture of fear and respect. Margie, leaned forth and whispered in my ear, "Congratulations, Ralphie, you're a pimp and a gun runner for the mob and I'm your main whore." Fortunately I know a lot about nefarious things as a part of me likes the dark side of life and the dark souls of life. I guess it's living vicariously.

"She wanted to know if you still could fuck," said Margie, and I stuck my tongue out and ran it around my lips in answer, and the old gal almost busted a gut laughing. But Margie shushed her and said I was dangerous and did not like jokes at my expense.

"Marge, tell her I'm a gun runner for the mob and am your pimp and that I have a Lugar strapped to my leg. And that I like to cut whore's faces when they get out of line. Tell her I am in a bad mood and feel like offing someone as I had a bad business deal and somebody's going to pay. It's Piranha chasing Piranha in here. Spy vs. Spy. Tell them enough that they can feel you're in "The Life" as the whore's call it. Then clam up as you're afraid I might go off. Keep her talking about herself," I said.

Marge did as told. So, her trashy reading all that crime fiction about criminals and serial killers is really going to pay off, I thought. "I know what to do, be aloof and make them come to me. They will come sniffing for blood and opportunity. You translate for me. See, that high school education has really done a lot for you Margie. Who knows to what heights you may ascend." I said.

"You're a smart ass, Ralphie, and after this vacation, I intend to enroll in college to get the damn English degree so you can't talk down to me anymore," said Margie.

"I know, I'm a real asshole, sometimes, Margie. I have a bit of the caveman in me that wants women to be subservient and meek. Which you are NOT. I like your fire, girl and I'm sorry if I'm a chauvinist pig but that's not all I am. I think you're brilliant, Margie."

"Well, thank you, Ralphie. I know you like the clash of wills, we have, the fighting and making up. Except we can't do all we used to do," she said.

"What the hey, Margie. We're criminals tonight. Let us go stealthily forth into the miasma of serpentine souls. Let's try to be fiendishly evil except not serial killer evil. We only kill people for business reasons not because we are thrill seekers."

"Sounds like a plan, Ralphie. Look at these women. They look like they were dipped in makeup and I thought I was the gaudy one. I'm sophisticated by comparison," said Margie.

"They all look like "The Brides of Chuckie", I retorted. "And the big hair makes them look like hydrocephals or water on the brain, such as they are. We're sitting here judging them, Margie, because we're white and comparatively upper class. We're Hob Knobbin' with the Hob Goblins. God says, 'Judge not lest ye be judged.' Let's just party hearty and not be so smug. They are, life forms, you know" I whispered.

"'Only an asshole would say that, Ralphie," said Margie.

"Curmudgeon is the word, doll. And we came to be with them. Invite the Madame over and her male friend. Say we want to buy them a round of drinks.," I retorted.

The couple came over and the chair creaked in protest as the fat Madame sat down. Her name was Carnival Louise as she used to sell cotton candy at the Circus before ascending the ranks. Her boyfriend, was the spitting image of "Don Knotts" complete with bug- out eyes, and fidgety mannerisms. He was her lover and manager. She had a stable of fifty whores and was making money hand over fist. She spent it like a shark in a feeding frenzy I gleaned. I began to really like them. I gave them the number of a financial advisor and told them to save for their old age and Louise laughed, busting a gut, so to speak. She said in French," I make the money and Fredo spends it on gambling. There will always be Johns and pretty untalented girls. As long as I give my cut to Nordstrom. You've got to know him. He runs everything from drugs, to gambling to prostitution to diamond heists. To not pay him is unthinkable. Surely if I ran guns I should know of him." she intoned.

Then she said saving money was foolish as we all died and can't take it with us and besides Fredo was an expensive toy, as she called him. Fredo puffed up like an enraged parakeet and slapped her hard across the face. Tears welled in her eyes and she kissed his hand and begged his pardon for being disrespectful. Fredo had her heart and her money and liked it just fine. He was like one of the little birds on a Hippo who eat lice from the animal's hide. And Ralph noted in his striped tee shirt he looked kind of like an Apache dancer.

Nordstrom, as it turned out walked in, and came over to greet Louise who introduced Margie and me and spoke of our occupation. Oh, but he was suave and sophisticated and intoned in flawless English why had I not let my presence be known to him if I was not operating in his area. His tongue snaked out and ran along his mouth like a lizard trying to catch a fly.

I answered that I was from the Italians, and worked out of Florence for Don Capella, known as Acapella, and that of course, I was just an lowly associate not a made man, and I motioned the waiter to bring Nordstrom a drink. He accepted, and said he had not heard of the man but would surely look him up if he went to Florence. He straightened an invisible wrinkle in his gray striped Armani suit and motioned me to light his cigar which I did. It's like when dogs turn over on their backs to show submission. And I peeled out three hundred dollars to show him how I appreciated his hospitality while in Paris.

He smiled, took the money and said in French that monsiour was most welcome to all his city had to offer and please consider myself his important guest. Later, after we went to our sweet red refuge of our bedroom, I dreamed of his gold tooth and his crooked smile, and how his colorless gray eyes looked not quite human. Staring, Staring, dead as fish's eyes.

Money Doth Make Bitches of Us All.

Sartre Was Wrong

Two dozen red roses arrived the following morning, with a card inviting us to an exclusive formal party at Nordstrom's estate. It was signed, "Affectionately, Lemuel." So he gave us his first name. I have never considered myself a dynamic nor charismatic guy, and I wondered why he was so impressed as I barely said two sentences to him. He probably knew I wasn't a gun runner nor pimp nor even a Mafiosi. He definitely knew our names and room number and he probably knew I was an IT man with computers and retired and dangerous as a fucking snail. What did he want with me. Okay, I'm tres literate, and know art like the back of my hand, and know all about music from opera to blues. I guess I am a cultured guy. Could it be I interested him for some reason which I could not fathom. Maybe he was after Margie and I damned sure hoped not. What a mess I had got us in. Not to go would constitute an insult. We had to go. I had REALLY FUCKED UP this time.

I have made an ass of myself. Yet, I do believe in God, and I thought I was being punished for being a wise ass curmudgeon. I really think people are nice just because they're afraid to show their real selves. Margie never did that: she's an original. Told me right up front she was a prostitute and not in an apologetic way. It was as if she had spoken Mr. Roger's stock phrase, "It's a wonderful day in the neighborhood." She named her price which was rather high and remarked offhandedly," For some reason, I trust you. I generally run a security check on my prospective clients, no beaters, scat artists, or sadists, or misanthropes.. Masochists are okay, though. What kind of sex were you looking for?"

I replied, "A reasonable facsimile of a girlfriend or wife."

"Oh, so we'll be bosom buddies," which caused me to look at those firm lush nectarines.

And she laughed aloud, "Are your eyes going to fall out of your head. You're not a virgin are you, hon?" I was about thirty then and told her "no" and we've been together ever since. Margie never edits what she says and has lost a number of friends that way. But you always get truth from Margie even if it doesn't favor her. I told her I had never been with a "working girl" before, and no whips or chains permitted. I must say that Margie expanded my imagination and showed me the joys of "role" playing. She was made for me and I was made for her and then there's this damn party. Godammit, I was beset with the problems of Job. I was screwed but not in a good way.

I have never seen a more sumptuous palace than that of Lemuel Nordstrom. And beautiful people abounded, long necked gooses of women with diamonds woven into their hair, alabaster backs, and heaving bosoms, faces out of Italian Vogue, with some French people but as the French are thin stressed out people with dark hair usually it's hard to discern ethnicity. The stars had deserted heaven and were on his landscaped lawn. Beauty and evil is a potent brew, and all eyes were on Marge and me. I wore an Armani tux and Margie had a gold sequined designer gown and diamonds graced her ears, neck and wrists. Her face glowed like the pale and silvery moon. The platinum blond hair of another woman caught most of the moonbeams, however. Angel hair on the devil's woman. A good compromise and Lemuel flanked by two blond starlets greeted me in person, and said, "How do you like my little spread, Ralph, and Marge you look splendid. I like a lush looking woman: women these days are too thin, not ripe like you, but know I do not chase my women and as beautiful as you are, it is not the business I wish to discuss with your husband. Enjoy yourselves, circulate. These are artists and people from the entertainment world, mostly European, I hardly ever invite my business associates to my fetes but there are some here. My advice, tell no one anything personal or you might regret it. Marge, you have the gift of a good listener, and Ralph, you have a lot of stones to come uninvited into my watering hole, my bar. Invent yourself, say you're a linoleum salesman like "George" on Seinfeld. Tell them anything but the truth. I shall get with you about midnight, and my friend, we shall talk. Then he departed with the attractive, blond gargoyles.

I said, "I want to be involved with toilets, Margie. I am a bathroom consultant from America. I sell designer toilets to the Hollywood mogels, you know like sinks with gold faucets and the like, and mercy, me I forgot my cards and may I have yours instead? It cracks me up when guys from South Philly say "terlet". I am the ultimate waste disposal guy, and you're my Brady Bunch wife. Are we agreed?"

"If I disagree, you'll make a scene like propose to me again and cry. The poor man in the wheelchair rejected by the red headed bitch. I know you enjoy playing with people's heads but you're not cruel only ludicrous. What do you know about toilets, Ralph?" asked Margie"

"I worked my way through college the first time as a plumber, Margie. I am just a muli-faceted jewel, Darling. It's bathroom humor. I think I'll be the bathroom buffoon then start talking about Satre and Nietche when they tire of hearing about toilets. I'm going to bore the shit out of them. Literally. Then switch into really intellectual stuff."

Why can't you just be a dentist or a shrink, Ralphie? My god, Johnny Depp is here with his wife. Oh my God. We've got to meet him, Ralphie, please."

"I can't darling, because like Frank Sinatra, I want to do it,'My Way'. Why don't you go sniveling over there and get his autograph on your tits? Oh, at the very least kiss him on the mouth and grope him in the crotch."

"Like Sartre, you are absurd, Ralphie."

"You read Satre, Margie. Do you agree?'

"No, and yes I did read him and Nietche, too. They're both world class assholes."

"That's my girl, always putting things into perspective, and yes, they are both wrong, wrong, wrong."

"I know, but can we go over to Johnie Depp. AND NOT DO THE SHIT ROUTINE?" pleaded Margie.

I agreed and he was very entertaining and kept trying to find out what I did. I was very vague and said I was a trust fund baby turned art patron. Then switched the conversation back to him while Margie drooled her chance away. She froze and said not one word to him.

As I left, I realized he thought she was disabled in the mind department but didn't tell her or make a fuss. What a sumptuous spread, Lemuel had laid out. Ice sculptures were everywhere,(swans and cats) with Dungeoness Crab legs and full lobsters. Marge always one to go for the visceral, had a medium rare steak, baked potato with sour cream and cold, asparagus tips with a giant piece of brie. Marge does not diet at a party or as she is wont to say, "How could it be a party, then." The tall, anorexic blond starlets stuck to salad and fish and did not get inebriated. Fear of the calorie is a heinous thing and a modern aberration. Marge is too full of vitality to behave that way. Hell, she's like the fuckin' Wyfe of Bath. I hoped she wouldn't get too drunk and ball one of the handsome male stars in the topiary maze. Margie is a wild woman when she drinks: the vapors go to her pussy. So, I went around boring people and watching them think of troubled departures, like "My wife has cancer and I have to go home now. Nice to meet you. Mr. Twilliger." I collected all these rejections like a kid collects seashells at the shore. Some were really creative like, "I have to go get my botox from my doctor now. He only works nights."

If you could see the gowns the women wore, it was like a painting by Seurat. Pointilism. Gashes of red, viridian, gold, bronze, silvers, blue, and for the vampiric ones, black that melted into the night. And the perfumes drifting in the air, a miasma of scents, bitter and sweet like red roses on the vine. They were all extremely physically fit: I didn't try to ascertain their mental states. That is like a rape, to prod them into agony. No, I'll never do that. I only know what people want me to know. I'm no spiritual vampire: I have my own warmth and light and don't need anyone else's unless they want to share of their own volition. I am a curmudgeon, I know, but there are some things I won't do. Sure, I play with people's minds but never in an injurious way: I keep it playful. I've got my own soul: why would I need someone else's. That's why Margie and I are such a good team. We don't feed off each other in violence and misery. We keep it light. And that's the way to have a good, spiritual life.

A raunchy raven haired beauty came up to me at precisely at 12:00 midnight and said Lemuel required my presence in the study. Now the mystery unravels, I thought. There were books of all kinds, the great fiction writers, philosophers, historians and one book on quantum physics. I looked well and filed it into a compartment in my brain: see a man's books and see a man's soul. This is a true maxim. Criminals are not criminals because they lack intelligence, at least those at the top. I asked if he had read them and he answered in the affirmative.

"Lemuel, why have you called me in here. What might I do for you?"

"Have you ever known a criminal who feared death" he asked and then stated, "You know one now."

"You're afraid, why?" I asked.

He threw his medical papers in my lap and I browsed through them. It seems Lemuel had MS. "I know all about you Ralph, and I also know you are a very strong person, and I am weak compared to you. You go around cracking jokes and making people laugh. And people love you. I had a family once but she got tired of my coldness. I just could not love her. I can't love anyone: I have servants, I do not have lovers, so to speak. They love my money, not me. And now I want at least, one sincere, warm relationship before I depart this earth. I want you to be my friend. That's all I want in this world and I don't have to tell you to keep my malaise a secret: you're a very bright man. I know you are very rich so I can't offer money unless that's what you want. And I don't think it is. What may I give you? Name it and it's yours. You'll die long before me," he said.

"There is something you can do, Lemuel. Look out after Margie and see she gets a nice man to marry her and no fortune hunters. You know the word, EuroTrash? Well keep them off her. Rich widows are always victims of these kinds of men. Keep them away from her and be discreet. Don't let Margie know you're looking out for her. She'd be pissed and it's true Margie is very strong but she is not infallible. I think for the most part, she'll be okay. It's my dying wish that she become an English major. I want her to use her brilliant mind: maybe become a romance writer. Or even, a real writer. She's very independent so don't clip her wings if she wants to fly. I want my Margie to have a good life after I'm gone and I know you won't have to force her to get the English degree. She's an honest woman and after this vacation, she's going to start taking courses. I owe my life to this woman: she never turned away from me though I was a real stingy curmudgeon. Now, I'm just a curmudgeon and I spend plenty on her. I love to see her face light up like it's fuckin' Christmas Eve. I never in my whole life deserved such a fine loyal and loving person. And Lemuel don't try to be her man. She's too fine for the kind of hardness you have inside. If you go for her, I'll come back in Zombie form and eat your brains while you're still alive and kicking. Swear on it. They say there's no honor among thieves. What is it you want from me?"

"Well, Ralph, I want the freedom to be with you as your friend and confidant."

"I don't do drugs nor alcohol, to any great, degree, so don't involve us in the people you know. I know you are like piranhas always trying to swallow one another. I don't want myself or Marge to have anything to do with your criminal life. I just know Margie is too trusting and half the time can't figure out when her friends are jealous of her. She just smiles and says the person was having a 'bad' day. Can you promise me that and how can I ever trust you? Don't make me a business associate. I will not give advice. I do not want to be a consigliere. Get me?'

"Oh, so you watched Godfather with Marlon Brando. How else would you know that word. I promise I won't move on her. I am too cold a man for such a hot, sweet temptress. I need women who will let me disrespect them and buy them off with money for the abuse. A mafia woman takes a lot of abuse. Because the job I do is so high pressure I need to blow off steam with someone defenseless who can't fight back. Margie'd be at me with the butcher knife every other day. I can tell she doesn't take abuse. Strength is all through her. She's a burning, white hot light and I'm a dead, cold star. I just want to be around normal people before I die. Normal people who don't want anything from me but friendship."

"Lemuel, I will be your friend and I will show you how to laugh at life. But you need to find your warmth or there's nothing I can do. I mean it. Life is meaningless if you despise yourself and others. Rouseau, said life is "nasty, short and brutish, "Well, it's not. AT ALL. Life is a candy store. And I want you to see to it that Marge is also in your will for a goodly sum. And Sartre was as big an asshole as you fancy yourself to be. Life is NOT ABSURD! Sartre was wrong. I have a blast everyday and sit around and think of goofy things. Here's some witticisms for you: Mobster eating Lobster, an Occasion for a Caucasian and my favorite, never make an enemy of an anemone. I think of silly shit all day and I'm writing a book of observations so Marge will always have a piece of me, after I'm gone. I record it on disk and don't tell Marge. It's a surprise. I can't really rely on my hands or I'd type it. It's called, I Could Have Died Laughing. Do we understand ourselves, Lemuel? You may call me friend. And you're right. I am strong." We toasted with Salignac. Strange bedfellows. Yes.

Evil Like a Serpentine Snake

Lemuel was a real trip. He flew in each weekend to see us, and never arrived without ponderous and wildly expensive gifts like designer gowns and rubies for Marge. Rubies are the most expensive jewels in the world. And he also gave her a multiplicity of other jewels, emeralds, diamonds even expensive Indian jewelry like bear claw necklaces, concho belts, silver bracelets and chandelier ear rings. And for me, a gift of Absinthe, and Ralph Lauren leisure wear. He always searched for the unusual, and things that would thrill us. It's no sin to love someone for his money: it would be a mistake not to. We became quite fond of Lemuel, and through vast experience he knew how to endear himself to people. Sometimes, he came laden with a bounty of eclectic food, cheeses and exotic fruits and melons, like Dame Largesse from medieval literature.

We came to love him. He was a monster but he was trying and that was quite poignant in a way. We knew he was an Arctic cold inside and we tried to warm him with our love. We included him in all aspects of your life, knowing that warmth and normal people have a palliative effect on one dying of his own coldness. I do not mean we included him in our sex life such as it was and Lemuel had the class never to request it. He respected us.

I will say in the beginning, he had to force me. When I turned down his proposal he said,

"How would you like an early funeral: I know some really fine undertakers and you do resemble Rock Hudson, so the makeup would be minimal," he said.

I replied that I understood his point of view, and that, Marge and I would be honored with his presence in our lives.

He laughed, and said, "So you saw 'The Godfather'. An offer that you can't refuse."

The odd thing is I could feel his sadness and the machinations of his reptilian spirit. Apparently, I'm am empath and silence has a voice which speaks to me. He was so evil he made Bella Lugosi look like one of those misty, hazy, Degas dancers. I have never experienced such rage, turmoil, and malaise. His mind was so alien to mine that it was a tumultuous and disturbing experience for me. I never revealed that I could feel him to Marge or to him, or to anyone else. I did what I do best, "Be Ralphie". I joked mercilessly, one joke following the other like dominoes collapsing in sinc.

He was always thinking of ways to best other people through finesse and pain. It was a different mind set entirely. His schemes were nefarious and frightening. I willed him to get into our way of dealing with life. To make everything a source of constant joy. Don't take that morning coffee as incidental: glory in it. You may be dead tomorrow and pay attention to weeds as they are a beauteous as a cultured rose in a private garden. Don't just eat, revel in what you eat, whether it's pancakes or expensive duck liver pate.

I had no doubts that we could warm him. We've met dangerous, evil people before yet never to this degree. I wrote a poem called, "Monster Hearts" which best sums it up.

MONSTER HEARTS
Monsters have tender hearts too long ravaged, ravaged, ravaged.
Hearts too long in the odious dark, afraid of the light.
Afraid of the warm, orange, singeing light of the triumphant sun.
Afraid to be loved and undone.
Just a fey package wrapped in bitter brine,
So afraid to be undone, undone, undone.
Hearts with secret rooms where none may tread.
Hearts with secret rooms closed to the silver
light of the joyous, trembling fairies.
Soft mist dying on the tangled, troubled vines,
Which nourishes hearts, hearts, hearts.
Yes, better off dead than to be loved instead,

To live in endless night, in a viscous purple mosaic of pain.
Nothing to gain, nothing but pain, pain, pain.
The night, a wicked sylph, with dagger in hand,
Guards a palace grand full of hearts,
Bleeding, bleeding, bleeding, and dead to life.
Hearts closed to life. Dead as nails, and
cold as the Great Arctic North.
No way to wander, take siege, and soar up to the cerlean skies,
And be kissed with a wondrous light of a thousand, sweet, silver stars,
Pin pricks of love in the endless blackness that is night.
Forever bound to the silent rooms, where none may tread.
Oh, Monster, Mine. Oh, Monster Mine, bound up in brine.

Well, I wrote that about a scheming wench, and impromptu succubus, Ophelia, the girl I was with before Margie, "The High Priestess" of Vitriol. She had to get vicious before climaxing, and in the beginning it was kind of like being a rollercoaster, with just the right air of danger. Exciting and invigorating. Then I began to tire of the bleed marks on my back made by her lionine nails and the soreness of my balls where she squeezed them. Then I said to myself, "Ralphie, get rid of this fuckin' harpy. She means you no good always talking down to you, and kicking you in the nuts". Then she cried and said, "Was it something I have done?"

Go figure. It was just an opening line on another Battle Royale. I told her she was the most wonderful chick in the whole world but that I was a closet gay. That kind of surprised her but the main thing is she packed up and left. It was a little bon mot of mine. Oh, yes, I have known some hellacious people, and my first instinct is to get away from them ASAP. Don't drink the varnish, Hon, though it would be a beautiful finish. Some people are just noxious, or radioactive, or deleterious like cancer cells, and such was Lemuel. Let me interject what he looked like. Elegant in dress, white blonde hair turning to gray, a handsome face kind of like the late Gary Cooper, and a swift way of moving like a large cat coiled to spring.

Yet, one could not help but like him. He was so charming. Yet, in this mind, he was always planning ways to best other people. To bend them down and make them suffer. I don't want people to suffer. I want them to be ready to be assailed by wit and humor. Me, I don't feel a need to dominate people. Life's a gas, I tell you, and I have decided to forfeit this vale of tears in gales of laughter. I want a goddamned wake when I go visit the ultimate CEO, Our Lord Jesus. I thought of some new rhymes: an antelope eats a cantaloupe, ambivalent ant, liver quivers, and you get hard more in Ardmore. You'll grin more in Bryn Mawr. I do know these are corny but I'm corny, so what must you expect? Oscar Wilde, I surmise. Then I thought of our mutt dog, "Your Ratness," who likes to pee on guest's legs, and hump on ladies with evening gowns on. I apologize but I do find it funny. I don't know why he does it but it always ends by me dragging him by the collar to a closed room or to the yard and his dog house which is modeled after a Tudor castle. I did the carpentry work when I wasn't yet sick. I think "Ratness" has a hard on for the human race, a curmudgeon dog, and that makes him invaluable. Also he likes to lick my cheek and it feels like a warm dishrag and not at all unpleasant.

Lemuel was going to waste him or it but I said, "First off, Lemuel, he does that to everybody except Marge and me, and it seems to me, you have poor impulse control. Sure, he's a pill, but so are you Lemuel. Funny as a motrician's wake. Don't you ever see the humor in things. I really don't know how you'll be when you have to wear diapers and someone has to spoon your food to you. Think on that, Lemuel. Don't sweat the small stuff. My dog looks like the late Winston Churchill and that's why I keep him around."

Lemeul replied, "Your dog, besides being more fowl smelling than a pile of cow dung, is a certifiable asshole and deserves to be dispatched."

"Don't you think that's what people think of you, Lemuel?" I said.

Next thing, I know, Lemuel's got his gun pointing into the middle of my forehead.

"Get that fucking gun off my forehead, Lemeul. You said you wanted to experience how normal people act. Well, normal people can say unpleasant things and disagree without coercion of any kind. The Golden Rule is important in my world, and is part of a happy life."

Lemuel slowly lowered the gun placing it on the kitchen table which Marge retrieved to unload the bullets.

"No fucking gun play in My House, Lemuel. Do you hear me?", Margie screamed, and being hot blooded, she slapped him across the face.

Lemuel picked up one of the bullets and told Marge to swallow it as a birth control pill, or at least take a bath.

I roared with laughter. He was learning. Margie laughed too. "Ralphie, likes me to bathe every other day. He says I smell more like sex that way."

"Well, you stink pleasantly. As or The Golden Rule and all the Thou Shalt Nots, I have broken every one of them. It's do unto others before they do unto you,' said Lemuel.

"Well, hon, you're in a different world now," said Margie, "And we shall not jump at your command, nor shall we be your servants. We are not your "yes men." She put her hand under his chin and kissed him lightly on the cheek to soften her words.

"Tigers are different than fawns, sweetie," he replied. "I am a great, big, nasty beast."

"Bestiality is not reality, Lemuel," I remarked, "but I will tell you Margie is a certifiable psycho and unmedicated. She prefers to see life in her own way. That is not to say she'd actually harm us if pissed. Yet, there was that one time she chased me through the house with a butcher knife. Psyche, Lemuel, I'm just pulling your leg about the butcher knife but our gal is a bit hampered, and you should know this. How are thing's on the Psycho front, Margie?"

"You both have snakes coming out of your heads and if I look you in the eyes, you'll be turned into stone. It's an old story. Psych!' replied Margie, who let out her raucous bray.

"No, really, honey, how do you feel?'

"I feel, hot and cold, like an old wheel barrow rusting in the wind. Unloved and forsaken. Give me some hugs, guys. I know I am not in reality."

We both hugged the lights out of her until she begged us to stop. And a crescendo of laughter emitted from the cavern of her mouth.

"I know what to do let's drive to the shore and have a picnic. I'll bake two oven stuffers, make potato salad, make a batch of mac n' cheese, a dark lettuce salad with grape tomatoes, and avocados. You two go out and get the wine and cheese and see if you can find two pies, apple & cherry. Get me some big bottles of diet cola as you know I can't drink. I'm reading Hemingways, "A Moveable Feast," in class now and this just seems like what to do. Does that sound like fun or what!" exclaimed Marge.

I said the quote I live by from the movie, Auntie Mame quote:

"Life's a banquet and most poor bastards are starving"

I'll take that as a yes," said Margie. "And Lemuel get out of that designer suit into some jeans. I swear you're brilliant but don't have sense enough to come out of the rain. As the blacks like to say, 'act like you know'".

The Picnic

S o we three, odd people went to the Shore, Atlantic City. Lemuel's drver took us in a black limousine, lean and mean. Marge loved the capers, Spanish olives and garlic flavored water crackers. Lemuel, and I proceeded to get wasted on champagne and Marge had one glass of it and no more. Our girl had nerves of steel. Lemuel made the off handed remark that he realized I was not like most people. I was not afraid to die.

"Nobody could ever control me, Lemuel. I leave 'em in stitches but you, on the other hand do too, only literally," I ventured to say.

Lemuel roared with laughter and said, "You're a real wit, Ralphie."

"I just like fooling around. When they come to stuff me in the coffin, I will have taken a bottle of viagra. What could be more obscene than a corpse with a giant hard-on. I want a wake not a funeral with everyone getting drunk and telling off-color jokes"

"You'll be fine, dear," said Margie "I know you still want to be buried in a speedo with little white, Italian lights blinking on and off, and one eye rigged to wink. He means it, Lemuel," said Margie.

"I never in my life heard such bull shit," retorted Lemuel.

"You've got to learn to roll, Lemuel. Life is a colossal joke and our Dear Lord is one hell of a guy. He has a huge sense of irony. Just when I turned into a good man, he gave me MS. You know, I fuckin' speak the King's English. Do you know the sheer will it takes to sound the way I do. Also part of the Grand Master's plan. Oh, he'll have me mumbling, and stuttering one of these days. Until then Carpe Diem and slainte. It's Irish for cheers. I was good and God dumped on me: you were bad and he fucked you royally, too. Go figure. None can understand the mind of God. Strange Bedfellows, my friend," I said.

Lemuel burst into raucous laughter, and replied that he thought it would never come to that. "Oh, so you have a sense of humor, after all," I said incredulously. "Maybe you'll evolve into a human being after all. Oh, shit, that was uncalled for. I apologize."

"You keep insulting me, ya' fucker. Why should I take any of this crap. Okay I'm a psycho, and I like it that way," said Lemuel.

"If you liked it, you wouldn't be here. You know you're missing out on all the things that make life great. Having warm and sometimes painful feelings is what makes us fully human," I said.

Marge butted in saying that I shouldn't push too much on Lemuel as he was trying, and to remember that one learns life's lessons best slowly. She said, "Don't ask him to absorb all your philosophical bull shit at the speed of light. You took a long time to see God's plan for you, why should poor Lemuel be any different? The man's s trying, Ralphie. You can note that by the fact that he hasn't capped you, yet."

"Yet?' There aint no yet, poodle lips. There will be no capping of me, right, Lemuel?" I said. "Thanks, Marge," he said, "and there will be no capping of Ralphie. I'm feeling things I never felt before, and now, I see what kind of guy I really am, and don't like what I see. Tigers have different priorities than lambs."

"You're nothing if not a great, great beast. I'm like just a regular guy who wants to get the most out of the time I have left, It's like The Seventh Seal: I'm playing chess with death, and I'll eventually lose. Hey, let's play a game of chess: you be "death", I said.

"Been there: done that," said Lemuel archly.

"You're going to cry like a little bitch when I beat you. I used to be a chess master before all this. Ah, then the splendor happened to me," I said.

"We'll see about that. What do you think, we, criminals do with all our time. Sit around with our thumbs up our asses. I win, you're my bitch: you win, I'm your bitch," said Lemuel.

On that day I lost to Lemuel and fell in love with Margie all over again as she moved my pieces for me. She was backlit by the afternoon sun light and it had the aspect of a halo and her face, in shadow, was robin's egg blue and her sundress was violent crimson showing off her milky white shoulders. It was in the manner of the Seurat painting of ladies with parasols and top hated gentleman strolling by a river. I watched the young men rowing in teams up and down the river and I felt as if I were young again and could do it myself. And Lemuel wondered what I could do to be his bitch as I was incapacitated. He said he would, however, hold me to it. He said I was already God's bitch and I laughed because it was true. So true. The brie stuck to the roof of my mouth and the cold raspberries died on my tongue, and the wine danced across my cerebellum, casting a warm, cozy haze about the world, and I felt like a pearl happily ensconced in an oyster shell. It was one of those times which remain in the senses like a haunting melody with all things soft edged and ethereal. When asked how long my "bitchhood" would last, Lemuel said, "Forever" and laughed. We began to enjoy our weekend visits by Lemuel and we incorporated him into our lives.

One of the stipulations of my bitch status was I would record the amazing tales of Lemuel's life and have Margie transcribe them into a book, and I was never to look him in the eye, unless told to. Other than that there were no stipulations. I had to play "submissive" yet I was still the grand instructor about things amazing in life. Margie had no such restraints and would stare into the coldness of his gray eyes to try and find the person within. She saw the pain lying under the coldness and I being an empath also felt his pain. This was a tortured soul, a man, carrying past transgressions and hurts around inside him. He was a fearsome beast, a murderer, a drug overlord, and a pimp. Yet aside, from his coldness, his wit was amazing and he'd have us howling with laughter. It was a new aspect to his personality and I could see this was the way to reach him through humor. He was delighted to entertain us, and I have no doubt it meant a great deal to him to have people who wanted nothing from him but companionship. And his gifts were amazing, a signed copy of Emily Dickenson's poems for Marjorie, a mega food processor, and for me audio books. I told him I was an English major "gone wrong, terribly, terribly, wrong". I remember his delight in making smoothies using bananas, strawberries, grapes and pears, and vanilla yogurt and milk. He held out a grape to Margie, one time, and said, "Have a grape, Suzette". He also made smoothies of raw vegetables like turnips, spinach, carrots and celery. So many combinations, I can't recall them all. Nobody could make smoothies as well as Lemuel. He was also a Cordon Bleu chef.

One time he made crab cakes, filet mignon wrapped in bacon, curried brown rice, garlic clove spinach, candied yams with ginger, cinnamon, and brown sugar. For desert, raspberry wine, and strawberry fruit tarts with melted dark chocolate at the bottom of the pie crust and home- made whipped cream. He was a master or epicurean delights. At other times he took us to exotic restaurants. We ate Moroccan food, Mexican food, French food, Greek and Middle Eastern food, and African food.

He once flew us to France just to have dinner In Louis XIV's palace at Versailles. It was a thousand dollar a head fete and no one could do enough for Lemuel. We even had our own waiter standing by to fulfill all our needs. It was a night for wine and getting inebriated. Ah, the linen tablecloths, the pale white roses dying silently in their vases, the paintings of Louis in all the rooms, and the pleasant, welcoming coolness inside the palace. That night we slept in Louis XIV's bed chamber. In the morning there was juniper and chocolate croissants, fresh squeezed orange juice, a gigantic fruit bowl, mushroom and cheese crepes, and the best coffee I had ever tasted. Lemuel warned us against revealing our identities to the many people he introduced us to. Margie was Lucille Leseur and I was Dominic Leseur and we floated on the river of entitlement. It's fun to be treated like royalty and everyone seemed determined to please Lemuel. He said he wanted to experience his world or at least the pleasant aspects of it. One of Lemuel's many concubines caught my eye. She was a lush six foot tall high fashion model. Her cheekbones cut arcs in the orange air as light streamed in from the lazy sun. Her eyes, wide set and large were a curious yellow color or perhaps they were chartreuse and her pouty mouth was the mouth that sucked a thousand cocks. Her hair was a glorious, natural platinum blond down to her ass. She was the kind of thin that runners are, muscular but not masculine. She wore a silver sheath and in her seven inch stilettos she was taller than most of the men except for Lemuel. He brought her over to our table and introduced her only as Magdalena. She was a submissive, I knew, from the way she never met Lemuel's gaze, keeping her eyes down cast.

She was delightfully French and seemed was genuinely happy to converse with us. My French is kind of rusty but Margie managed to translate for me, and looked a bit miffed at being outclassed in the beauty area. This is hard to do for Margie resembles the late Ava

Gardner. I never could stand a homely woman. It's not what you think: it's how you look that matters.

I know I'm shallow but who'd you rather bed, Mother Therese or Marilyn Monroe. Get my point, that is not in a "necro" way but if they were alive. I never much understood necrophiliacs nor serial killers though I do study serial killers. I can't study the necro's because it is an affliction few people will cop to, and there are no creditable witnesses. It's kind of a silent aberration. Personally, I think serial killers fail to develop a conscience or a human identity. They are like cock roaches, or leeches who feed on live matter. Man, I am just the king of digression. Oh, well, fuck me.

At the end of the scrumptious meal, Lemuel excused himself and called over his driver with instructions for him to show us Paris, the "secret Paris". and then at seven o'clock drive us to the Eiffel tower where he and Magdalena would join us for dinner. I took one final glance at Magdalena and I got the image of a long stemmed white rose.

At seven we met Lemuel and Magdalena and right away Margie, and I noticed the pink trace of a hand print across her lovely face that would eventually turn into a black and blue mark. Yet, she was painfully even more radiantly like a falling star from God's heaven. She noted we were alarmed and gave us a quick shake of the head and put one finger to her lips, the shush sign. We were careful not to say anything nor to challenge Lemuel who put one finger on the bruise and made a sign of a kiss on his lips. Suddenly she nipped at his finger then blew him a kiss with her full shapely lips and her laughter was like the sound of a fork hitting fine China. She moved painfully slow but without shame or fear and her chartreuse eyes were like bits of a flame flickering in the hushed, still air. And she was tres charment and guided our conversation so skillfully putting everyone at ease but Lemuel. She spoke in broken English but her vocabulary was anything but mundane. She was like a queen holding court and even Margie warmed to her. She flirted outrageously with both of us. Lemuel, in silence, was purple with rage and his hands were clenched into fists. He preferred silence in women like the quaint machinations of a Geisha, and Magdalena was not having it. She ignored his discomfiture, and doubly increased her witticisms and her words were like raindrops hitting a tin roof, mesmerizing. Such an odd reedy sound was her voice and we perceived that this was a very powerful woman. Finally Lemuel slammed two thousand dollars down on the table and rudely informed her that her presence was no longer required and that she had bored his friends to tears. She stiffened a split second, then with elegant ease, shook our hands and expressed her joy at meeting us, and blew a kiss to Mon Homme, as she called Lemuel.

"Get the fuck out of my sight, Maggie. You disgust me?" Lemuel could not tolerate brilliance in a woman and we both knew he couldn't break her for she was already broken. It was there hiding behind her bravado. We also realized that Lemuel needed rage and misery to engage in the sex act and that he would always return to her, perhaps even kill her.

She smiled her radiant smile and sauntered out, turning halfway out to tell this joke,

"Tell me, mon homme, why is Frosty so popular.?" A long awkward pause that deepened the flickering white candles ensued. Then Magdalena drew herself up to her full height, stage whispered, "Because he was such a cool guy." Her laughter floated in the cozy dining room like something diaphanous, white curtains blowing in the wind. She had tortured Lemuel as he had tortured her. How do I love you. Let me count the ways. Let me count the ways.

Balls for Christmas

Well, I confess Christmas is my favorite season and Margie is a knock out in her dark, green, velvet bodice hugging gown trimmed with white rabbit fur. Lou Rawls is singing "It's Christmas Time, Pretty Baby" and we have Louis Armstrong on next, reciting "The Night Before Christmas" in his raspy voice. In fact we have a lot of black artists like the Temps and the Four Tops singing R&B songs of the season. Lemuel has joined us and Magdelena would join us later when her plane from Paris touched down to be met at the airport by Lemuel's driver. Mohammed arrived a day ago and he and Margie have been cohabiting like a den of rabbits. It filled me with joy to see that faint roseate glow Margie gets on her face and boobs after she makes love. She looks like a painting from Vermeer. And of course, I do sit in at times and I sometimes get hard. Sometimes.

With the bruised image of Magdalena at our last meeting I take Lemuel into my study with two snifters and a bottle of Salignac brandy to add fire to the anticipated flame and he gives me permission to call him "Lem". I am a student of human nature and I determined I would make a fine graph of his mind which was probably as circuitous as an Escher drawing. I already knew he was a psycho and a sadist. Fortunately Lem was rather flattered and pleased that someone would try to understand him rather than just fear him. He was vastly pleased with the self revelations which came forth as we talked. He seemed to take a perverse pride in his ability to manipulate and destroy people yet he did know he was missing a whole range of emotions and he hoped that I would be able to help him feel them. I have never known a sociopath as I am an empath and can read people like most people read books. I feel the ambiance of the person in my guts: it's like I can detect malevolence wrapped in a smile. It's like some people can always predict earthquakes because they are reading a seismograph. Well, I have one in my head. I always rejected these kind of people. But this time, it was a chance to see one up close and personal. I guess I have a latent dark side. I read books on serial killers because evil fascinates me. Shit, I hate to admit that. Well I'm dying in milliseconds, inch by inch, hour by hour and now I slur my words. Lem enjoyed the probing because for the first time in his adult life he was with someone who had no ulterior motives and wanted nothing from him. Lem was not the kind of man to entrust another person and especially a shrink. To his way of thinking he was not insane: after all, he didn't run around amok.

I knew in my heart that this was my last Christmas as I had to take oxygen day and night as my lungs were failing and I had twenty-four hour nursing care as Margie could no longer handle things. So, I wanted to make it the most splendid Christmas ever. Lem announced that this Christmas was his gift to us and he paid all expenses. Mohammed, the college student we met in Aruba, was also present. Lem was floored when I told him he was a special Christmas gift for Margie. He just couldn't fathom it declaring he would kill anyone who even looked askance at Magdalena. I asked him if he ever really loved anyone, If he did he would want for them what they wanted for themselves.

He paused, sucked his teeth and then said "no" but declared he loved sex, lots of sex. Magdalena was the only one who could please him or understand him for she was acrimonious and truly fearless, dressing up in a dominatrix leather bustier with eight inch stilettos, fish net hose and a cat of nine tails. She would whip him and verbally abuse him and this was the game they played. Then he would become enraged and beat her almost to the point of unconsciousness and then take her brutally like a bull in rut. Also he required her to recite French curse words throughout until she could no longer speak and he would say over and over again, "Die, Bitch, die." He laughed and said probably one of these times he might go too far and actually kill her, screaming at the top of his lungs, "Feel this, you Bitch, you cunt." And then he threw back his head and laughed. Then on a more serious note he would hate to 'break in" a new girl. He knew his impulses were aberrant. But he knew this in his head not his heart.

And I asked him how he would feel, and he replied that he would be sorry to have to break in another girl. That no woman he ever knew was as riveting as Magdalena or as strong in personality. To further elucidate, he remarked that he paid her thousands and thousands of dollars and was putting her through the Sorbonne as a chemical engineer and that he gave her a palace to live in, and allowed all her friends free access, painters, dancers, actors and scientists. The only requirement was that she could take no other man. Women were fine though as Magdalena was bi-sexual.

He further stated that he would never again find a woman as enchanting as "Maggie".

"She keeps ridiculing me as I beat her pushing me to the edge and she never begs for mercy. Maggie has but to ask something of me and her wish is my command. You see I cannot love without hate and vice versa. I love her in a place I cannot reach and she knows this. She is the most powerful and erotic person I have ever known," said Lem.

"But, Lem, you say you might kill her. That's very disturbing to me. Really disturbing. Margie is highly sexed and yes, I am jealous by nature but this arrangement with Mohammed makes her happy. Don't you want Maggie to feel safe and loved. I bet you even told her you might kill her," I said.

"Magdalena is my most powerful obsession and possession. She is a work of art and has the fine art of the Geisha. I rescued her from a brothel in Tokyo. The Yakuza are not gentle with their women and she had many clients. Now she only has one. I saved her life. I would never let any women of mine fornicate with a nigger," said Lem.

"Lem, you may not call him that. He was a prince in Nigeria and is a student of foreign languages at U Penn. In my presence, you may not use that word. He's got more class in his little finger than you have in your whole damn body, and furthermore he does not abuse women. That's not something you can be proud of, Lem," I said.

"Do not test my limits, Ralph or I shall morph into someone you don't want to know."

"Lem I am not here to offend you. I thought we were having an honest tete a tete. I ask you not to insult Mohammed, and not to abuse Magdalena" I said.

"Fair enough. Is this how regular people act? Just say the first thing that pops into their heads regardless of the consequences. You've read

Nietche and brother, I am here to tell you, I am the Super Man. That text was meant for men like me. Fuck your middle class morality."

"No, is the answer to how regular people act. That is a characteristic most people don't have. I always say just what I think. Chips fall where they may. Margie has oft had to smooth ruffled feathers and she's good at it. Do you want a fuckin' yes man, Lem?'

"No, that is why I picked you. You are really fierce. You would have made a good gangster if it weren't for your damned conscience. The White Man's Burden. Whatever. I have no such compunctions," he said

"You call being good a debility?"

"Yep."

"You are an ass-backward, holy shit bastard. Do you get any joy out of life at all."

"Sure, when I come out on top in my business deals, or kill someone who wronged me. Or when I dupe a rube like you. It's not personal. I like you fortunately for you."

I said that was like a complement from Lucifer and we both broke up in laughter. Then we joined the tree decorating ceremony in the main living room. The tree was a thirty foot silver spruce supplied by Lem. He also had bubble ornaments, old fashioned icicles and little, exquisite, porcelain red birds and blue jays to put on the outer branches but first we strung about a hundred little white Italian lights. The eggnog was a sweet tang on my tongue. And Magdalena arrived in a long sliver evening gown shimmering like the night stars in the heavens, with a mink stole draped over her thin shoulders. The back of her gown ended in the crack of her ass. Margie darted her an evil look then walked cheerfully over to welcome her in an embrace, and a small peck on the cheek. She had the aspect of a thirties movie star, and green was the perfect color for Margie as she puffed up like an angry hen at every pronouncement Magdalena uttered. Lem was quite amused at the crackling atmosphere and I did nothing as it was in God's hands. Maybe.

Christmas Eve

Margie is a Christmas freak and I just let her do her thing, the huge tree Lem brought us gave a festive look to our living room. Plus Margie Put Holly and berries on the stairwell to the upper rooms and was playing Christmas R&B 24/7 practically. She was basting a turkey, ham Cornbread stuffing, candied yams with ginger, cinnamon and nutmeg, mashed potatoes, green beans almondine, asparagus tips & asiago cheese and mushroom macaroni, and this did not include the pies she baked, pumpkin, apple and cherry She also baked a cinnamon, raison coffee cake for the morning breakfast cake. She put elves, angels and Santas up on the fireplace with pine sprigs and Christmas balls on the tables and mantel. The whole house smelled of food and the crisp smell of live greenery. We drank brandy and champagne which sizzled in our glassware. Red ribbons and candy canes were festooned about. Marge wore a red velvet sheath which accentuated her ripe body while Magdalena was resplendent in a gold lame jump suit and high spiky matching shoes. They were fuckin' angels from celestial heaven and you could give a shit to know what we, men wore.

Though we usually opened presents in the morning Lem insisted we open his on Christmas Eve. Though Lem did not love people he knew how to make them love him. Yes, he did. He could seem to emit warmth though it was not a genuine warmth just a semblance of it. A more generous man I have never seen. He was very astute. I don't care what people say. It's the spirit not the gift that matters. Friends this is bullshit. Money makes people happy like a hostess twinkie, all sweet and gooey.

He gave me a brocade robe and matching pajamas and expensive fur lined slippers from Nieman Marcus.. To the girls he gave precious stones, rubies for Margie and emeralds fo Magdalena, matching earrings and necklaces. To Mohmmed, he gave a signed copy of Isak Dineson's <u>Out of Africa.</u> How beautiful were the dangling emeralds from Magdalena's milk colored skin and platinum hair. Margie glowed like a very hot fire all in her red velvet and rubies. They can say beauty is not important in a woman. Another lie. It's the package not just what's inside. Yet Magdalena had a preternatural, or ethereal beauty while Margie was of the firm brown earth. I knew Margie was the last woman I'd ever have and I loved her all the more for it. She was still a helluva dame kind of like a fifties movie star. And she had this overwhelming sex scent wafting through the air with her Shalimar perfume. Mohammed was a dark flame with his blue black skin and white, white teeth flashing as he laughed. Mohammed had bought us all authentic African caftans. And for our house he also brought an African fertility goddess with the exhortation to rub her belly if the women wanted to get pregnant.

Margei said, "Oh, hell no, I'm not the maternal type. Give me dick but no babies" and she laughed that big old belly laugh of hers.

Magdalena said, "And I have my big baby who requires all my attention and care." And she embraced Lem with a faint touch to his cock. Lem was sitting on our Rococo red and white divan and she went and sat in his lap, and kissed him deeply on the mouth.

Margie then pulled me close and said, "The voices are back telling me to kill you or myself. I'm sorry this happened on Christmas, Ralphie. I'm going to be Mama Santa for two days. Then I'd better go to the hospital. Okay, Sweetie. I can be dangerous as you already know. I'll sleep with Mohammed tonight. He's stronger in case I go off. Take him aside and explain as best you can. He's an educated man and he should understand." I told Mohammed and he came and put his hand on Margie's ass and gave her a kiss. Good man, that Mohammed.

I went back in the living room, and Lem and Madalena were having a kissing contest. And I had a "gay" thought that he must've had a hard on and I laughed out loud to be going homo at this stage in the game. Marge came in and saw that Lem was feeling that I was being adolescent and prurient. She explained that I had a strange mind and was always cracking up over something and that I meant no disrespect.

"Yes, I know he has a strange mind and that he is fearless and sometimes ferocious. That's why I like him so much," replied Lem.

"That is a rare thing for Lem to say, Ralph, I've known him ten years and have yet to receive such a declaration," interjected Magdalena.

"You are suis generis, Magdalena, one of a kind. A truly fierce, indomitable woman. That is why I love you," said Lem.

"Mon homme, you have never told me that. I thought maybe you did on account of your generosity, I knew you had this really deep painful thorn in you which made you unlike other men." said Magdalena. "Lemuel, I am so honored."

"Don't make this a soap opera, dear. Not everything is in the public domain," replied Lemuel.

"You'd rather talk about your enemies as they are so numerous," she teased.

"The less you know about a person, the better. As they say, Familiarity breeds contempt. Never get too close to a flame: you might get singed," replied Lem.

"That's what men said of me before I met you, Lem," replied Madelena.

"Well, you are quite voracious, at times. Like a lioness," he said. And Margie asked what kind of woman was she herself. "I perceive you to be very solid. Very beautiful and vibrant, trustworthy and non manipulative whereas my Magdalena is serpentine. You are quite like your man only you have more subtlety. Magdalena is more criminally inclined, my type of woman. I like the bitter and tart. That is to say I like harlots. Smutty, lowdown and dirty in the soul."

"Merde," exclaimed Magdalena, "If I am those things you have made me them, bastard."

Lemuel slapped her hard and said, "Don't contradict me."

Palph, was up in arms, "Goddamnit, no hitting of women at Christmas, Lem. I mean that absolutely."

Mohammed was up in a flash. He caught Lem under his collar in a choke hold. "Hit the woman again and I pulverize you. I am much stronger than you, spiritually and physically, and I don't have to harm some poor harlot to feel my power as a person. The person you

hate most is yourself: that's why you take joy in hurting other people. You prey on those weaker than you to feel like a man," Mohammed said hotly.

I pulled Mohammed off Lem, and said the most inappropriate thing I could think of. "Why just can't get along?"

Lem, laughed and coughed deeply, "What the fuck are we third graders", and he turned to Mohammed, there is a moratorium for Christmas, Little Black Sambo, and you shall pay the coinage of your life for this affront."

"Racist! My ancestors were Kings while yours were toothless peasants out of a Breugel painting, tilling the fields. I come from a long line of Kings, and, we, have our ways of dealing with miscreants. You, sir, shall be the dead one. You shall never find my medicine pouch. I have a poison which kills real slow so you can ponder your lousy life then poof! Out goes The Eternity Dream. You did fancy you'd live to a ripe old age, non?" said Mohammed.

Marge burst in, "What the fuck, you two, threatening each other on Christmas Eve. You should be ashamed to disrespect my hospitality especially since I'm hearing the voice again. It says to kill you all, and arrange your bodies on the couch and have high tea, and do all your voices myself. Aint that a Bitch? And don't forget I'm the cook. I suggest you send Magdalena to watch over me and see that I don't put any varnish in the stuffing. I haven't yet but the impulse is there. Actually I want to kill Ralphie more because of those fifteen years he had me convinced he was a file clerk and we had to be in a horrible apartment, and I had to buy my clothes in Wall Mart. I'd kill all the rest of you for being 'material' witness but not Magdalena. She belongs to the SOTRF. The Society of the Royally Fucked. Darlings, I am a paranoid schizophrenic, and I do mean that."

"You let your woman live in poverty when you were a rich sonofabitch? That is so wrong. I'm shocked, and ashamed for you Ralphie. There's a special hell for misers. You go around hungry and can't get enough to eat or drink and you'd have sex with eighty year old whores. Old pussy stinks to high heaven and you would be a "slave" to their erotic whims, and you'd never get a change of clothes nor a bath. You disappoint me, Ralphie, you really do," intoned Lem.

And you casually say that one of these times you might kill Madalena. Kettle calling the pot black, if you ask me," replied Ralph.

Madalena, went over with tears in her eyes, and bitch slapped Lem, calling him a bastard, and she cried her eyes out figuratively speaking. Marge gave her one of the drowsiness pills so she wouldn't feel bereft.

"I am alone in the world, and the man I love desires me dead. I cannot abide this kind of life. I have tried to be so strong. I feel like Piaf singing for supper on the mean streets of Paris," said Magdalena.

"Magdalena, I swear it was just a slip of the tongue. I would never hurt you to that degree. Don't I bandage and putt my special ointment on you after our sessions. Aren't I solicitous enough," asked Lem.

"I will never touch, you, again. Lemuel. Sleep in your own bed alone until Hell freezes over. I am tired of your love and your hate. I can bear it no more," responded Magalena. "You've had me as your love slave one second over limit and I am breaking free. I shall be a chemical engineer as I graduate in June," retorted Magdalena.

"If you live to see, June, Babes. Nobody says no to Lemuel and lives," he said.

"Lem, correct me if I'm wrong you have made a 'terrorist threat' in a room of people who don't give a shit about your money and what you can "do" for them. Does that not establish a criminal trespass. We three are going to stand by Magdalena. Nothing shall happen to her in or out of my house," I said.

'I'm just talkin' shit," he replied. Magdalena then ran sobbing into my arms and Mohammed, and Margie did a group hug and the tears flowed like Niagara Falls. It's painful to experience good as it is to experience evil if one has not had kindness in a long, long time. It's kind of like having the sword of Excaliber thrust into ones entrails.

"Does, this mean Christmas is off. I promise, I give you my word as a man, I will never harm Magdalena. Maybe I like being around real people and I still have a lot of goodies to give you in the trunk of my Limo. I know you can't love me but please don't shut me out. I'm begging here, Ralphie," said Lemuel.

"Don't beg, Lemuel, you may come and go as you like but from his day forth I enjoin you not to have sexual congress with Magdalena. You had her for ten years: Let her have her own life now and keep paying her bills until she gets her masters degree. Agreed?

It chagrins me, but yes. I promise, said Lemuel."

"I am thinking there is no honor among thieves, said Ralphie.

"Give me a piece of paper and I shall write the accounts of my off shore earnings in the Cayman Islands and I shall make Marge the executor of my estate, and power of attorney. Does that impress you with my sincerity now. I don't want those crooks to get my money.

Maybe you and Marge could set up a clinic for MS clients. Watcha say?" asked Lem.

Margie rushed over and gave Lem a big tongue kiss and pressed her body into him.

What the hey, once a whore; always a whore and I wouldn't have it any other way. Merry Christmas, Gentle Reader, and don't forget to put out cookies and milk out for Santa so he can intuit you're not naughty but nice. Love those homemade ginger snaps! Oh, God I could just die I am so happy. No wait a minute I am dying. How soon they forget. Ha!

Christmas Morning

Well, it was now Magdalena's duty to keep watch over Margie. At the end of the day Lem would take her to the Farm of Funny. Lem seemed gennuinely concerned about her condition and Margie, God bless her, still had the Christmas spirit mixed with her psychosis. She brushed by me and whispered "Merry Christmas, darling, I'm going to kill you if it's the last thing I do." I said, "I know, baby, but wait until after we unwrap our gifts. Does that sound plausible, doll?"

"Yes, Ralphie, then I can festoon you with wrapping paper and ribbons as you gasp your last ragged breathe. I am going to garrote you with my cowgirl belt," she said.

"I see, well, I'd rather you pop me with some heroin. Ask Lem, doll, he's a drug lord and will have access to that substance. After all, death should be pleasant and peaceful. Then I could just slip away into LaLa land. Does that sound like a plan, Margie. Am I not a doll baby."

"Ralphie, you are a gem and we can't all be gems. That's exactly what I'll do. In the meantime I'll make the coffee and the mimosas. Why is Magdalena following me around everywhere.?" asked Margie.

"I don't know, doll, maybe she's into you?" I ventured.

"Oh, no, those butch girls really like me. I did a Lesbian floor show when I was hooking once. I kept thinking of pomegranite's as I was eating her. She fucked me with a big black dildo from the back but in the right hole and I came like mount Vesuvius. Then I collected my money and blew the joint as fast as is humanly possible. Yes, lesbians are a persistent and persnickedy lot. Once they get a crush on you it's all over for you. Do you think Magdalena is besotted with me?" asked Margie.

"And who wouldn't be besotted with you, my sweet lush peach?" I said.

"Well I'll just have to grin and bear it. Pun intentional, Ralphie. Ralphie, did I ever tell you I loved you?" she asked. "Well, I lied because I'm going to cut off your damned cock and balls, you hear me, motherfucker?" Margie screamed.

"Well, dearest, let's wait until after breakfast and open some more gifts from Lem, okay? Time is not of the essence. 'Take it easy baby, cuz I worked all day and my feet feel just like lead'. Elvis Preasley, one of your favorites," I remarked.

Magdalena walked in like one cool drink of ice water and led Margie back into the kitchen to finish making breakfast. Ever so gently did she impel Marge to leave me alone.

They prepared a real repast, Mushroom and cheese omelets, bacon, sausage, grits, and that delicious coffee cake Marge makes every Christmas. They also prepared an excellent fruit bowl, with berries, melons and green grapes. Afterward we adjourned to the living room and began opening packages. We got Lem a costly and ornately carved chess game and some Polo shirts in tasteful muted colors for Lem was tasteful above all else. To our surprise, Lem got each woman a complete wardrobe from Nieman Marcus, from lingerie to matching purses and shoes. To us, the men, he gave tasteful Armani suits and shoes to go with them. Mohammed gave Marge a trunk of exotic cooking spices and for Magdalena, a complete selection of Victoria Secret Lingerie in her size which was six. For the men, he gave us erotic enhancers like rhino horn, and various expensive herbs. It was capitalist over-kill and we loved Lem for his generosity. He was glowing like one of those green wax Jesuses one sees sometime around Halloween. Margie was on her manic upstream and chattering like a magpie and not making any sense yet no one corrected her. She was our poor, lost baby orphan or our idiot savant. Yet they knew she could become violent at any minute and so everyone was really watchful keeping her away from knives, scissors and other pointed metallic things. Margie became so disorganized that Magdalena had to put up her wardrobe from Lemuel and pack her luggage and Marge kept saying, "Please, Magdalena, don't go. Don't leave me with those misogynists. Keep Ralphie away for me. He wants to destroy me." Magdalena took Marge in her svelte ivory arms and looked into Margie's eyes with her clear chartreuse orbs and told her all would be well and that she was going on a little vacation to rest for a time, and gave her a sweet, sisterly kiss on the cheek.

Well, we got to the Farm of Funny or Shrinkorama at half past two: the place was one of Lem's suggestions as it was very expensive and resembled the mansion out of "Gone With the Wind." "Tomorrow is Another Day". My mantra and thank you, Scarlet. Their Nurses were so sweet, I almost thought I was on a soap opera. They embraced Margie on both sides, and Mohammed proclaimed he would be there for her to. She said "Good, at least you're not like that cocksucker, Ralphie. I'll kill you, you sonabitch," she screamed. But the attendants held her firmly and gently. I was glad of it as Margie is preternaturally strong when in a manic state. There's always a little flair up every ten years or so and it's always about "Killing Ralphie." I think this all had something to do with when she was a hooker, cruel pimps and such. All men get tumbled into the category of one, cold hearted bastard. She'd have to cry it out or scream it out. Magdalena, though a hooker, as well, seemed immune to abuse, or she was made from tougher stuff than my sweet, dangerous Margie. I marveled at the sheer force of her personality, so deep and serpentine was she with just the right tinge of evil. I imagined a viridian halo around her lush platinum blond hair like the Bibical whore Mary Magdalene. It was Lem, I worried about, whether he'd really set her free because of his admission that he might go "too far" with her. Could Lem be other than what he was, a vicious, grasping evil piece of shit. I would work on Lem. Perhaps there was hidden some aspect of what is human in him. However, so far, I had not found it yet. This was a man who never could never grieve, feel spiritual love, or have sympathy for another person. He was so charming, so slick, even scared old ladies would trust him. Girl scouts would adore him. On the surface he was like any other waspish, well dressed gentleman. I had to secure Magdalena's safety for he would only escalate in violence until he killed her. Yet, Magdalena really liked Lem, perhaps loved him, for rescuing her from the Yakuza. In my mind it was from the pot into the fire. Perhaps at some level she knew this. Yet Lem came to her infrequently and he gave her the life of a princess. Magdalena was ennurred to riches, glamour, and danger. She was a tigress, fascinating to know, unconquerable, and witty as any comedian. In fact she loved stand-up and would crumble into laughing hysterics when she saw a funny man. Lem himself had a noir, wry sense of humor and loved Alfred Hitchcock movies. Lem even called him "Fred". He was also a fan of David Lynch, the Cohen Brothers, Jon Waters and Fellini. His favorite films were Fargo, Reservoir Dogs, Pulp Fiction., and Amarcord.

How would I help my ailing Margie? How would I save Magdalena from an almost certain death. I was only one man. I knew Lem would disdain "life coaches" and "New Age Philosophers." Lem was as black as obsidian inside: there literally was no light. Nothing remotely human. He was a "Force to be Reckoned With." What had squelched the light inside him. What? Lem was like a Rubix cube. Whenever I asked Lem about his parents, I got a noncommittal, "They were fine people". Then silence. Dead silence. When I asked Lem for the happiest times of his life. Lem would reply there were none he could recall but he liked winning, ergo power. Winning was the most important thing to Lem. To dominate and sometimes humiliate the people who crossed his path. He saw people as objects to serve him. I knew I would have to find an Achilles' heel, and it was almost impossible. But one day, Lem remarked that his stomach ulcers had healed since he had taken up residence in my house. That meant he could feel our spirits to a limited extent.

So on the other hand he could sense the dark spirits of his cohearts, and this made him ill. He knew his world was poisoning him. Therefore, he was vulnerable, somewhere. I surmised that he knew he, himself, was a toxic personality. Where there is darkness I can make light. GODAMNIT! I AM THE GREAT RALPHIE AND I SHALL PERSEVERE.

"Listen, Lem, we're going to the shore. There's this bearded fat Lady I want you to see, and Magdelena can come too."

"She's on a jaunt with my, or shall I say her, credit cards. Nothing could draw her away from that. She's preparing a gourmet meal for tonight, and, no, I'm not going to fuck her," said Lemuel.

"In my current state, I don't want to see any corpses yet on the other hand I plan to be one. Did I tell you my funeral plans. I plan to be buried in a spedo with a giant erection with blinking Italian lights, with one eye rigged to wink. And it's going to be a wake, a fucking celebration of life. Margie knows all about it and will arrange all the food and liquor. You can say clichés like "He's in a better place" and the like and my friends will laugh their asses off. You be the straight man.

I got a whole impromptu stand up. People are to tell jokes and laugh. That's how it's going down. Be a mench, Lem. Don't play head games on my friends. Don't do that. Get your trunks and let's hit the road."

When we got to the boardwalk, I dared Lem to fuck the Circus Fat Lady, and he laughed, a real belly laugh. "I'd rather fuck a corpse that's been two weeks in the woods."

"Lem do something for a dying man. I request you to fuck her in her trailer. Give her a huge orgasm," I said. "No rough stuff either."

"Okay, I'll do it. You think $250 would do it?" said Lem.

"Oh, a lot less, This 'Lady" has not takers, trust me." I said. Afterward, Lem came out with a big grin and said, "I actually enjoyed it. It was so REAL." The 'Lady" came out all flushed and flashed us the A-okay sign and she was laughing like a hyena. It was a real Diane Arbus moment.

"What's the dumbest thing you ever did, Lem."

"I ate a mouthful of red fire ants on my brother's dare," Lem replied.

"Ouch, must have hurt." I said.

"Okay, I know what you're doing, Ralph, Looking for my weak points. Something to explain me, my condition. There are no reasons. I just didn't have the same drives as other boys did. I liked to hurt small animals and butterflies. Burning them. My brother for the most part avoided me, and my parents were the same. They were ashamed of me and ashamed of themselves for their failure to socialize me. They were both shrinks. Sometimes people are just bad. Ralph."

"You made that fat lady so happy, Lemuel. You're not all bad. And you're laying off of Magdelena, that's a positive thing. The right thing to do." I said. "I have to say you are like an angry ant you climb over corpses of other bugs to sting your mate as you fornicate, and It's a rhyme, lord of crime," I said.

"That's a highly unflattering portrait. Yet, as I go further, I see you can look into me like no one else could or was brave enough to do. I just acted and everyone acquiesced. I like the look of blood on fair skin, and I like to look at people suffering. It makes me feel powerful, and I get the feeling that that is when I most possess them. I have a need to possess souls."

"I know that Lem. Frankly, I've got to commend you for not trouncing Magdalena anymore. You're doing the right thing, Lem, as you admitted your shortcomings, and that is a far journey into humanity. You are learning kindness and common decency. The man I first met would have never made, nor realized, such an admission," I said.

"Don't think I am completely reformed, Ralph, I just like being around you and Margie. It's like watching the old Ozzie and Harriet reruns. It's warmer inside me, yet I know I could still kill at the drop of a hat. Or, moreover, arrange to have someone killed. That's not going to change. It's who I am," said Lem. "I wonder how Margie's doing in the Farm of Funny. How is she?"

"Well, it's going slow. She said she loves me but thinks I would be better off dead…by her hand," I said.

"How do you stand it, Ralph. I never knew a "mental" person before, or, at least in the traditional sense," said Lem.

"Well, what can I say, Lem. You play the hand you were dealt in this life and besides, I love her. She's quite a sensible woman when she's her better self. You play it as it lays, Lem."

"I couldn't take all the drama. Magdalena would never crack up like that. She's too hard, and yet, she has this faint glimmer of softness. For that I love her, and for the hardness, I love her. I see I am a danger to her so I'll never touch her again. I guess it's like the Christmas Carol, and you three, are like the three ghosts that visited Ebenezer Scrooge. And may I say 'Bah, humbug?'" said Lem.

Margie at the Farm

Marge found it extremely difficult to be incarcerated during the Christmas season. It was her favorite time of year and most of the souls inside were suffering from "the Echoes of Me."

They were drowning in self absorption, the constant churning of souls, like a snake trying to swallow its own tail. Marge was all right except for the ponderous wish to kill Ralph. She got dressed up each day in full make-up, cologne and eschewed all meals but one. The others sat down to the hearty meals and tried to fill the hole inside and mute their own agonies by gorging on food. Marge used to watch them eat with glutinous gusto. One wretched witch of Irish descent always said everything thing was "Delishuze." Her long, unwashed hair hung down like a forest of evil and food disappeared into the black maw of the mouth. It was disgusting to Marge to watch her, yet it held some repulsive allure to Marge, who could not understand her own fixation at watching this display of gluttony. It was like a passion play, or staring at a wreck on the freeway. It was the amazing how many of them, well into their forties or fifties, were still blaming their parents for their difficulties. It was, at any rate, not a malaise that love could cure for they were immune to love, and yet, desired it more than anything else. It was, as Margie realized, a lose/lose proposition. You have to love yourself first, then the love becomes available to another party. They did not love nor trust themselves, and were wallowing in pain like hogs in mud. Margie loved her own delicious self and knew somewhere inside she was a bit broken, and that it was no one's fault. When one grows up one takes responsibility for one's own condition and Margie knew it was up to herself to "get well." She liked the staff for wearing white. White conjured up a bubbling white glass of milk or a shy cloud in the cerulean sky. They were mostly black and Puerto Rican and as Marge knew they viewed themselves as "shepherds of their flock" and that is what they were. There is something comforting about being around normal minds when one is in transit from insanity to sanity. A long ride from the edge of life, forlorn and fearsome, she endured it, and began to knit herself back together like any good seamstress. She felt that most of the patients did not clearly perceive the meaning of life. And that meaning was that it was blessed to endure, and one must create a silver lining. They wanted to lay down their burdens and rest from the terrible pain they were in. Marge thought, "This is the place I come when I run out of petrol" as the Brits are wont to say. Marge was out of what it takes, yet, she knew she would be all right. She knew it was because she was warm inside, and they, the others, were subzero inside. Mental illness is largely an intolerance to struggle and pain interspersed with bouts of self loathing. Margie tried to lighten their loads with blasts of her bodacious, bawdy humor. She told them what one tampon said to another. "I don't like you because you're all stuck up." And she told them the following joke. You have a group of ten jackasses and then you take one away. What do you have left. "An-Ass-in-Nine." She got their stories, collecting them like the tales of E.A. Poe, gems of grizzly horror, back roads winding into nothingness. A world like an Escher drawing. A girl trapped between two lesbians forced to make love who said, "We all get abused." She said it like that was in the center of her being. And Margie knew to put that on the outskirts of town with the rats gnawing on old bones. These things had to be vanquished and accepted. They could not be fought for that would be reliving the pain. To relive past pain, like the re-looping of film, over and over again. This was their lot. Reliving sorrow and pain and angst. People think mental illness is contagious and that is why the ill ones are shunned. And it is contagious. Broken spirits engender malaise and emptiness in others who are not strong. The strong can tolerate the broken ones but not everyone has the strength nor should they. Life is a joyous and perilous proposition. Live it up before the lights go out. That was her motto, and in healing others or trying to, Margie healed herself. She never asked them for the contents of their souls nor did she waylay them with tales of her once tawdry whoredom. She kept it light, and they often sought her out to live in the shadow of her warmth. Margie was full in herself, and she got well by basking in her own warmth.

The New Years Party was a shimmering, ethereal, sexual miasma for Margie's home coming. All, the major players were there, and I, Ralph, strung a crepe sign saying, "We will not Kill Ralphie" across the kitchen door. Margie brayed with laughter when she saw it, and she hugged me, and told me of her time in the loony bin, and went around saying "Delishuze" to everyone. She was so glad to see everyone, even kissed Magdalena on the mouth, a tongue kiss. Then she did a Rita Hayworth impersonation, of a women in jail movie. She grabbed the back of a chair and said dramatically, "I want to Live!". Margie, even thinner, wore a red satin evening dress with high silver strapped shoes, and black lace panty hose while Magdalena, wore a long chartreuse lame evening gown with matching high heeled stilettos. The guys, me, Lem, and Mohammed, wore what the hell you think we wore…black tuxedoes.

Picture an Edward Gorey scene, women thin as wraithes and distinguished gentlemen in waiting, and an ice Falcon surrounded by all manner of shrimp, lobster and Dungeness crabs. What shadows the chandelier cast on our faces, partly in dark and partly in light, like our spirits. The red color of Margie's hair was like a flame in the light while Magdalena's hair resembled nothing if not spun platinum. How the champagne sizzled in our glasses, as conversation ebbed and flowed like the tides, then later the expensive sherry we drank with our seafood meal resembled vampire's blood in our cut crystal glasses. After a while Margie disappeared upstairs with Mohammed, and we heard the sound of his hands slapping her ass, and her sighs of lust. Lem looked nostalgically at Magdalena and he ran his hands, lightly down her bare back as if counting the bones in her spine. They paired off, to my dismay, yet I spoke not a word. I sat in my chair prison and saw the Christmas tree melting with my tears. Oh, the reds, greens, blues, and silvers and gold. Ah, the dying slowly of the Christmas, tree. Even as I did so. To hold a blizzard of memories to take with me into the nether world.

Hooray for Lemual

My shining hour' was when I came downstairs to see a resplendent Magdalena with no bruises and Lem was jus beaming and looking for my commentary "Well, then, Lem does this mean you have changed," I asked

'No sadly, Ralph. I' m the same reptilian bastard I always was but I can control my rages, and will stop taking them out on Magdalena. As I have formerly admitted I was using her to work out tensions of my job on her. She is delighted," said Lemuel.

She shouted, "No more, Mister Bad Guy and I have you to thank for it, Ralphie. Lem was gentle with me as one would be with the petals of a rose." said Magalena.

"I have never felt so close to a human being than I am with you, Ralphie. You see into people and yet, you do not use their weaknesses to harm them. I have taken a page from your book, You understand I cannot change what I am only how act. That I can do. When I see you get more out of life with soft feelings, I know I might not get there, ever. But, I will act that way to make my woman happy. In fact with you people, I genuinely want to make you all so happy, Even Mohhamed. I can get him a job in a Fortune 500 company when he graduates. There is always demand for linguists to translate. I see what makes a man like you great. Your humor, your warmth and a simple and genuine benevolence. I have never met a more fun guy. Even in your direst hour, you'll go out laughing," said Lem.

"Of course, Life is a gas, and anyone who says different is full of bull shit. Lord, that incarceration with the lump of uglies, had sure made

Marge horny. She told them she was a Santeria High Priestess and would cast a curse on them if they tried to rape her. Margie can get creepy weird when she wants to. Fortunately, this is a seldom aberration. I am surprised she did not break the bed or bang her head on the headboard and get a concussion, she's so horny and Mohammed not me gets the benefits. Qulle domage." I said.

Margie and Mohammed descended the stairs with looks of mirth and satiation and Margie wrapped her arms around my neck and lambasted me with a series of wet kisses on the mouth and neck. I could feel her boobs pressing against me like two soft kittens, and I remembered the days of Margie and me and how we made the headboard bang against the wall. I remembered her opalescent body gleaming bright in the moonlight like a white ghost, the being between her lush pink slit. We were a fearless symmetry envied by jealous Gods and then I got sick. I got sick to please Him. Then I laughed at myself, sitting their maudlin with memories and past madness. We explored each other's bodies like spelunkers in a cave and now Margie was with Mohammed and it looked like he would marry her when I was "gone". "Gone but not forgotten." "Deader than a door nail" "Happy in Heaven". I thought of all these clichés and the final cliché, "Gone with the Wind." And I laughed my ass off. And everybody just kind of looked at me like I was insane which of course, I was. This is nature's way to let you know you're a wrong one, and the joke has played out. It is nature's way of letting you bear the pain. Insanity is not all bad, folks. I suggested we go to the video store and rent up a shit load of comedies, and have a movie marathon and everyone was in accord. Margie wanted the old Rock Hudson and Doris Day movies like "Pajama Game" while Lem wanted the more morbidly funny, like Reservoir Dogs & Pulp Fiction, as was his taste. I wanted all the old Alfred Hitchcock movies. Magdalena wanted Felleni's Amacord, while Margie wanted the sequels of "Monk" whom she said reminded her of me. Yes, I am a clean freak and yes I put coasters under people's drinks and wash my hands about fifty times a day. In my well, days I used to wash my dick off with rubbing alcohol after having sex unbeknownst by Margie. I have a morbid fear of germs. I'm dying slowly and I'll be damned if I let anything beat MS to the punch. Ergo, I am still a clean freak. It's why we have a maid three days a week, every other day. This wouldn't be so bad if Lem did not pay her to "suck" him off. Since making it with the circus "bearded" lady,

Lemuel discovered he liked odd and ugly, and our maid was both and about sixty years old. I think life is strange or at least mine is. The best kind of life to live is a strange life. And you may quote me on that and avoid dull people like a plague. They sap one energy source: they are the black holes the physicists blather about. Lem now says he wants to ball Siamese twins and preferably to have one of them be gay. I don't tell Margie all of our conversations: she has an intolerance for the really, really bizarre. Lem is more about taking me aside and talking to me about his life.

Things of weirdness, and I'm going to quote him here, as much as I can remember. "I love the way that old slut smells like dead people on a cool metal slab" (reference to our maid). On Siamese twins, (he wants one of them to hate sex and the other to be a nympho). And I'm sure with his money he can arrange to have this little scenario. He thinks he turned criminal when he killed the family dog, a French Spaniel. "I had to do it. I felt the dog knew what I was really like. So I put rat pellets in its food and mom and dad were mortified and never spoke to me about it, but they knew. They avoided my little peculiarities like the plague. They figured if they could just wait until I was of age all would be well. I don't know why I like hurting things but I just do. I was like Ralph Ellison's Invisible Man, only not black. It was like I never existed. I used to be enraged that they did not love me. But fair is fair, I did not love them either. And my fucking brother was like 'Wally' on 'Leave it to Beaver'". Lem was never loved. Small wonder that he did not know how to love. But I know he loved me. He never admitted it but I knew. He loved all of us, for the first time in his life yet he could not show it save for the lavish and tasteful gifts he showered on us, Mohammed included. Mohammed was the most stable of all of us all, and he had a warm honeyed down to earth wit that we came to adore. Always he was as steady and constant as the morning sun and he loved my Margie almost as much as I did. He came and went out of our lives as his studies took him to Philadelphia, (he was in his last year).

I knew that this was to be my last year too so I determined to keep up the jokes and pranks I usually played like giving the our aged maid candy underwear for Lem to eat and I laugh now just thinking of it. What an odd banquet. I bought Margie a slew of Victoria Secret lingerie to wear when she made love to Mohammed. Generosity is what life is all about, and laughter. I became bed ridden in February and could not sit up without assistance. I had round the clock nursing care and slept under an oxygen tank, and Margie would come and lie by my side until I went to sleep at night. And Lemuel would come each day and talk to me of his life in crime and sometimes he would do standup comedy, one of his favorites. It was like comedy noir. It was quite funny in a menacing kind of way. I lost the ability to say words and the hand of death just lingered above me. I knew my time was coming. One day Lem rented "The Seventh Seal" where a man plays chess with death to prolong his life and avoid dying. And as he left me for the day he pressed a chess piece, a knight (horse) into my lifeless hand. I smiled in as much as I could and he wiped the tears from my eyes with his linen monogrammed hankerchief, and gently placed his hand on the side of my face, saying nothing. As Lem spoke I made up in my mind the looks and expressions of his clients and his soldiers from the colorful, exacting way he described them. It was like a constantly playing movie in my head and Lem seemed to know how grateful I was. This monster was being kind to someone for the first time in his life. It was as if Lem was my creation, and I felt proud. And I felt safe in the presence of this strong, fierce man. As long as Lem was talking I could not die, or so I thought. Well, the curtain closed or as in the old time gangster flicks, "It's curtain for you, Ralphie."

And now I am in the miasma of the afterlife, and Margie lies like white shell in the black arms of Mohammed in the marriage bed and late at night she cries for me. I guess I can truthfully say, "Now you don't have ol' Ralphie to kick around anymore." Nixon said something to that extent and I always thought it was funny. Lem, the murderer, drug dealer, criminal par excellence had saved me from the pain of death. He gave what no other could.

THIS IS RALPHIE, YA CLOWNS OVER AND OUT

Erasmus Vermouth Serial Killer & Artiste

By

CAROL ANN

Chapter One

Erasmus Vermouth was nobody's sweetheart. He was thin and gangly and so weak he could barely open a jar of peanut butter. He had a sunken chest and a dowager's hump and his arms and legs put one in the mind of pipe stems and his face resembled a plate of tapioca pudding, so nondescript were his features. His preternaturally luminescent, robin's egg blue eyes caused some to look away quickly. It was like seeing a six car pile up on the freeway.

Erasmus was a ne'er do well, thirty year old man living at home with no intentions of getting a job. He spent his days in earphones blasting Black Sabbath and Pink Floyd heavy metal CDs. He had a drunken, welfare mother who nagged him relentlessly about his lack of ambition and drive.

"Turn down that crappy music," she yelled, "and get a fucking job." His response was to turn it up even louder. She avoided ever coming into his room because of his pictures of woman's torsos sans the heads. When asked about them he replied he was "a tits and ass" man and she was lucky he wasn't queer.

A brief description of dear old Mom (DOM). A morbidly obese woman who wore cheap faux gold jewelry, ear rings that said, "Jackie" on them. As if people would see them and they would think, "Ah, there goeth Jackie, a marvelous woman." She stayed drunk on beer and pizza, and to his credit, Erasmus looked after her and kept the house pristine. He was a neat freak and a germaphobe.. He was anal retentive as Freud would say. There had never been a "father figure" in his life just a revolving door of scabrous losers his Mom brought home from bars when she was young. Then when she got fat the "uncles" ceased their visitations. DOM bathed only twice a week much to his chagrin, and he had to bath her as she was too fat to take baths without help. Her long Gray hair reminded one of a witch from Grimm's Faerie Tales. Her smell was like that of old garbage or rotten pussy.

One day, melancholy overtook her and she made a confession to Erasmus that he was not sired by European Royalty. His father was one of nine men she balled at a "Crisco Party" in the mid-sixties. "Crisco Parties" where the participants rolled around on a Crisco slathered floor balling complete strangers. When she got pregnant none of them would "fess up". Then there's always the old fifties saying, "No man wants used goods." As for DOM she had a dim notion that something was really wrong with her son but like life itself she blotted it out with liquor. When she tried to discuss the pictures on his wall, grizzly headless female torsos, he would retort angrily that she was trying to "get inside his head" and storm out of the house. As it was she really liked his neatness and she was grateful for his help for at 400 pounds she could not take care of herself. The shit hit the fan, however, when he brought a dead puppy home DOM had a conniption fit.

Erasmus, you killed Skippy, Mrs. Arnaut's dog. She's been calling him all afternoon. Why'd 'ya do it?" she asked.

"Dunno", he said and broke into cackles. He shrugged it off and slammed the door to his room.

She made him take the dead pup to the dump late that evening. And got to thinking how much Erasmus liked dead things, and how his face was expressionless unless it was for dead things, and he blushed bright pink when he held a dead bird. He had a childhood taxidermy kit and had mounted and stuffed over two hundred birds in his lifetime. She would have thought, "Thanatos" if she had a smattering of knowledge which she did not.

On the other hand, Erasmus, was brilliant she thought. He knew all about literature and studied college level medical texts especially about surgery and anatomy.

"Erasmus," she would say, "you should try and be a doctor."

And he only said, "Nah, jeus suis artiste. I want to be an artist like Andy Warhol. It is my destiny. Don't be so plebian. I feel I am destined for greatness."

"Fat chance for that. All you do is lock yourself into your room and listen to hard Rock. Listen, it's time for you to get a job. I've sold the house and you have to move by the end of the month. I'm moving to Florida.

Before she could say another word, he clouted her on the head with a rolling pin, and said to the thin air, "Those who live by the rolling pin. Die by the rolling pin." As the light fled from her eyes, he felt a full erection and he came like Krakatoa.

And he thought in amazement, "So this is how I am."

Chapter Two

T hen he sobbed and said, "I'm sorry, Mommy. You're really not dead are you. Oh, please. Come back, Mommy."

This was when he got his Greek Chorus. They were the popular girls in his high school class, pretty in a cheerleader kind of way. Bottle blonds with pert turned up noses and cotton candy in their brains. True All American Princesses.

"Euw, ill. You offed Mommy Dearest. Killed your own mother. Lizzie Borden gave her mother forty whacks and when she was done, gave her father, forty-one." Insane shrill laughter.

"Shut up bitches. You know I didn't mean to," screamed Erasmus.

"Ah, temper, temper. We're going to be right with you now forever, you perv. Ha! Ha!"

"You are the Bitches From Hell." BFH. And he began to cry and pace the whole night through arguing with the BFH.

Toward the dawn he cradled her bloody head in his lap and told her softly to come back alive. "Does she know you came in your pants when you killed her. Otherwise, you're a dud," said BFH.

Then he got a brilliant idea. Why not preserve her for all time. Render her fat with acid, treat her hide with salt and bring back her youthful self. In short, he would immortalize her. Then he would always have DOM. After all, he loved her in a sad, needy way. It wasn't as though he had any friends.

The BFH screamed out, "You killed her and there's no way you can put it right. You evil perv. Turning her into some kind of human doll is atrocious."

Erasmus ignored them and began to work on DOM. He shaved her long, matted gray hair off and replaced it with a big hair platinum wig which he sewed to her head and he salted her hide to cure it before re-hydrating it and cut away spare skin to fit a size six Dolly Parton form. She was quite a beauty in a Diane Arbus kind of way and she looked truly eerie in the light of the silver candelabra he had placed on her dressing table.

He kissed the top of her shell like ear and whispered, "See, you're not really dead, mommy."

Then he heard her voice again. "No, sonny, I'm not dead. I'm alive in the same way Marilyn Monroe is alive. No, wait a minute Marilyn is really dead. Would I be talking to you in this way if I were dead?"

"I am so sorry, mom."

"Oh, it's all in a day's work, Erasmus. I forgive you in the way Jesus forgave Judas. Look how beautiful I am. Say, I want a cigarette to celebrate my new found youth."

Erasmus thought better not to disclaim on the bad effects of smoking. It seemed a moot point.

"You know I'd never do anything to hurt you, mommy," he said. An eye fell out of her socket and he gently replaced it.

"No, doll, you never would. Sweetums plant a little smoochie on mommy's cheek, por favor. And he did, recoiling a bit from her pungent death smell. He then sprayed her with Tea Rose perfume. Ha had dressed in a chartreuse peignoir to look fetching.

She looked ghastly in the half light of the candles looking like a cold slab of whale meat, with one eye listing to the side. Erasmus lit all the candles to remind DOM of the time she was a concubine to a sailor in Monte Carlo and this kindness was not lost on her.

"This reminds me of my time with Pierre AlsaceLorraine," she said, "It was a happy time, no? I broke his heart because in the end I had to take up with his Captain. More money, you know. I had to think of you and our general welfare. I never loved anyone again more then I loved Pierre. One cannot be vivid and not break some hearts."

"Yeah, you were a real killer when you were young, mom."

"Don't I know it. I made a living taking money from men. Did you really think they were your uncles and that I was a shaman curing them from witches' curses."

"That's what I thought until I was about thirteen. Then the other kids at school told me you were a whore," said Erasmus.

"Do you still think money grows on trees in Hawaii?" she asked and laughed.

"Definitely," he said.

"Now, Erasmus, you tell the realtor I decided not to sell and that I'm going to nurse my sick sister back to health. Remission from stage four cancer. Keep it light. Simple, and don't elaborate. Tell the same story every damn time. Be in a hurry, important meeting to attend. And tell them I'm in a better place."

"That's pretty droll, mommy."

"Sure, just like my quest for your success and my future grandkids. I know you're screwed up about women and wish I could help. Son, you've got to have money if you want to be with a woman. It's the most important thing above all else."

"Ma, let me work on that my way. I have a rare condition which must be addressed first."

"Okay. I have vowed not to nag you anymore. A promise I will probably break," she said.

After this brief respite the BFH started up again. "Deader than a doornail. Deader, Deader, Deader. And now he talks with her as if she were reincarnated from the dead. She is risen, risen, risen. Just like Anthony Perkins in Psycho. We can't hear her: so she isn't alive and it's only you talking to yourself. You are answering yourself. Dumb psycho fuck. Whatever."

It was not long before DOM began her long, ludicrous harangue, calling him a shiftless, no good stick in the mud. "If you're such an artist where is your product? Where would Van Gogh be if he never painted?"

"My taxidermy is my art. Like in your case turning a sow's ear into a silk purse…" he said.

"It's like the sound of one hand clapping if nobody but you knows it, Erasmus."

"I am percolating, just waiting for the water to rise, mom," he said.

"What a crock. You've been percolating your entire adult life, son. I've got the solution, you're good with the dead, why not be a mortician? You already look like you've come from a funeral. Or, better yet, be an animal taxidermist. Try something, anything. Just get the fuck out of the house," she said in her whiny voice. (Like chalk on a black board).

So he got sick of it. "You'd think death would improve her" he thought bitterly.

He tried out for mortician and was told he would not be strong closer though he had the face for it. "You see, son, we are in the world of fantasy and we sell the fantasy that we can make the dead comfortable and happy. On the highway to heaven, so to speak," said the oily headed caretaker. "It's illusion we sell for a price. And that's where you come in to convince them to spend high for it. In reality they're not any less dead for fifty dollars. Sorry, you're just not a salesman type. I hear they're hiring at MacDonalds."

Erasmus hurried out and to release tension he set a number of public trash cans on fire. So quick he was as to not get caught. Erasmus was so indistinct: he garnered no attention. When he got home his mother was so excited.

"Erasmus, I've got you an interview at Udon's Taxisdermy World. His name is Don Udon. I screwed my courage to the sticking point as that bad Lady MacBeth said. See, I do know my literature. I'm not as ignorant as you think. It's one of the biggest outfits on the East coast."

"Did you also ask God to unsex you hither if you know Shakespeare so well. I am not going, mommy," said Erasmus.

"You are to. You will get your artistic ass out the door tomorrow before one o'clock. The appointment is for two. I am not hearing how you're not going and take your entire collection of little dead birds and hawks."

"Screw your courage, mommy, and screw you," said Erasmus, close to tears. He then wiped a tear from his eye. "Nobody wants me, mom. The story of my life."

"Erasmus, he is most eager to see you. I told him how you began as a child and that you're very talented."

"I'm talented, mommy?" You think so?" he asked.

"Momma didn't raise no fool, Erasmus."

Erasmus aced his interview. Don Udon hired him on the spot. He fell out when he saw the birds exclaiming that they looked Like Japanese woodblock prints. He offered him a starting salary and the chance to do big game animals. He told him he would buy his first big game kit.

He then said he would train him but expected him to develop his own distinct style and that he was the future of taxidermy and that Erasmus would take taxidermy to "a whole new level".

He came home walking on clouds and waltzed his dead mother around the room. Then he tongue kissed her. Our Boy is a trifle weird.

This really set off the BFH. "Euw, ill, you tongue kissed your dead mother. Euw, Oedipal. Creepy. You'd like to crack open a cold one. Gross, you want your own mother!!!" For once they didn't affect him: he was so happy.

"Of course, dear. You can do it. Those birds look like they've got a heartbeat," said DOM. "Oh, my boy is gonna be a big success. I am so proud of you. Doll. Give your old mommy a big smoochie."

And he gave her another tongue kiss. "God, your own dead mother is trying to entice you. Euw, ill, ill, ill," they trilled.

"Oh, mommy, you are so bad," exclaimed Erasmus. "I kinda think we better stop. I don't have an Oedipus Complex."

"Well, there's more where that came from and you like 'em dead."

"Mom, you're scaring me. This is kinda like a Vincent Price, movie, Fall of the House of Usher, by Poe. I can't think of you in that way. Not really."

"Mommie knows best, Darling," and ran her tongue over her lower lip.

"I can't do that even if you were alive, Mom, and you're not, you're dead."

"Precisely," said DOM with a big grin. Erasmus ran out the door, and into the street.

Chapter Three

Erasmus then recalled how his mom would always come into the bathroom when he was taking a shower in his teens and how she would offer to wash his back to make sure he got "clean."

"Oh, go figure, my own mom after my ass. Sheesh, I got problems, Big Time."

Despite, his domestic problems, and playing the absentee son with his mother, and locking himself in his bedroom every night, he flourished on his job and was promoted after only three weeks.

What Don Udon didn't know wouldn't hurt him. Of course, it was too bizarre to tell. Erasmus managed to get a night position so he worked alone. He was alone with the dead things and he was in heaven. All the lovely dead things. Before he disposed of their innards he was getting into the vat with the organs of the animals, kind of bathing in all the death and he sang show tunes while he did it. "The Hills Are Alive with the Sound of Music." Then he would get cleaned up and dispose of the waste leaving no trace of what he did. Then he would wear the cured hides, growling and crouching around like an animal in rut. He wore their heads and looked out of their eye holes to see as they saw. He felt as they felt. Saw as they saw. It was a transcendent joy that filled his heart. He had their power for as long as he wanted. Then he would stop and do a brilliant rendering of whatever animal he was working on. No one captured the animal's spirit better than Erasmus: he imbued his creations with fire and blood, with ferocity and vitality as if they were alive. But the god, Thanatos, was ever present and Erasmus began to seek more dangerous game. Human prey. Women of flesh and blood. The only thing was Erasmus was too weak to overpower his prey in most incidences, and his skeleton key purchased from a comic book did not open any doors. Mostly he pretended to be a Boy Scout Master on a cookie drive which worked well getting him into their houses. It was particularly effective on matrons of a certain age like the forties and older. He chose women who could be literary characters or women who looked like Greek goddesses, or Renaissance images of master artists like Bottecelli's Venus.

His first "client" was Miz Mamie June, a larger than life, ripe, vibrant women of ebony black. He figured she could be a character out of the film, Chaka Zulu. He had on his Scout Master uniform, and wore an innocent benevolent expression on his face. He told her he was saving the youth from joining street gangs. This resonated with her and when she went into her purse to retrieve her cash he put his belt around her neck in an attempt to garrote her. She merely bent double throwing him over her head, then she brained him with a cast iron skillet. Before he blacked out he saw little stars and Tweetie Birds.

When he came too, he saw double and noticed he was bound up at the wrists and ankles.

"Boy, you are possessed by the devil and we gone do an exorcism on you and free you from The Devil," said Miz Mamie June. "Reverend Ishmael Ponders, will be here shortly with Brother Will and Brother Raymond."

The three kind faced black men came in like Good Shepherds, kind and powerful and they doused him with water from the Skuykill River blessed by the good Reverend.

"Devil, git behind me. I call you out like a scalded cat. Free this child of God from your evil grasp. Free him, in the Name of Jesus Christ and of the Holy Father." And there was a laying on of hands and a group recitation of "Free him in the name of Jesus Christ and the Holy Father. Free him, Oh, Lord."

The cadences of their voices enshrouded him and for hours he was exhorted to give up his soul to the Lord and to be washed in the Blood of the Lamb and did he know that Jesus died for our sins and he replied that he did. "For the Lord so loved the world that He gave His only begotten Son that who believes in Him should not perish but have everlasting life. Do you believe in The Lord, Son," intoned Parson Ponders.

"Yes. Yes, I do," croaked, Erasmsus.

"You know want I think? I think you are a blasphemer, a liar, an opportunist! To take advantage of a good Christian women like Mamie June who only wanted to help you."

Erasmus started to say something, But the good revering screamed, "Silence, blasphemer. The Devil has you in his sway. Fornicator, thief of conscience, murderer, iconoclast! Child of the Devil, may your bones rot in hell because that's where you're headed. Your brains gone boil inside your head and you won't have one minutes rest or peace. Not one minute! There is no rest for the wicked. And worst of all, he'll talk to you all the time. You won't even have your own thoughts. Is that what you want?" Is It?" he screamed. "Git thee nigh from this poor boy's spirit. Get out, Devil, I cast thee out. I cast thee out!"

This went on for abo0ut four hours, and Erasmus felt a gentle kind of peace descend on his usually nervous soul. And he thought vaguely of Little Richard. Then they dosed him again in holy Skuykill River water, and he convulsed with exhaustion. They, of course, thought he was cured.

Mamie June who was a nurse bandaged his head, kissed him on the cheek and told him he had to go to The Church of the Lamb of God, her church or else she would turn him in and she handed him his wallet to show she knew who he was.

And that was how Erasmus Vermouth became a Christian. Yet the dark god Thanatos still had Erasmus in his thrall. And he learned never to take his wallet on these exploits.

Chapter Four

Destiny doth make fools of us all… and more so for Erasmus Vermouth. His second attempt at being a serial killer failed miserably. He started by stalking a woman with a Renaissance face. It was her face that propelled him into a frenzy. He had to reinvent her into Botticelli's Venus on the Half Shell. The face and body were an almost prefect rendition of that famous painting. The thought preyed on him like a ravening wolf. All his waking hours were consumed in thinking of her. Her face was an oval like an egg: there was nothing of the hard edged androgyny of a modern fashion model. It was like a fresh peach in tone: so soft and feminine it was, as to make other female faces to appear masculine. She was a warm person and generous with her smile. He adored her despite his tortuous night dreams of taking her life. Her presence permeated his consciousness like a cloud blocking the sun. He tracked her.

by day as he worked at night and he never missed a day

Then, one day he saw his chance. She got out of her old Renault and one of her grocery bags broke spewing cans all over the lawn. He put on this best shy guy, benevolent soul face and he helped her in with her groceries. He had surgical gloves on which she noticed and he said he had a contagious skin rash condition. Then when she turned to offer him a freshly squeezed glass of lemonade, he put the cloth saturated in ether over her face until she quit struggling and lost consciousness. He then gently laid her on the couch as he prepared to inject a fatal dose of hemlock into her veins. He used hemlock because he thought it was classy to use a medieval remedy to life. Unfortunately, she was immune to the ether and she woke up, kicke him in the nuts, and started chasing him around the living room while brandishing a large, serrated butcher knife.

"I'm gonna' gut your like a Carp, motherfucker. I'm gonna' do what I think you'd do to me. I'm gonna' bake your heart and scramble your brain with eggs and onions. I'm going to use your intestines for chitterlings just like the black people make and last of all, I'm gonna mount your head on a plaque. How do young like me now, motherfucker?"

She was screaming at the top of her lungs, and Erasmus was really scared, so scared that he started bawling and blubbering nonsense. He barely made it to the door with her a close second behind him. She chased him down the street, screaming, "Motherfucker, I'm gonna' kill you, and you bawling like a little bitch. You make me ill. Some serial killer, you are. Don't you even know you're not supposed to cry. It's poor form. You think Heidnick or Ed Gein cried? The answer is a resounding NO. I'm gonna' find you and kill you. Bastard. Even if you get away from me this time."

Erasmus turned down Tremble Street, a dead end street, and ducked into a fortune teller salon. He alluded his Bottechelli's Venus and gained his Dame Largesse. The gypsy was not so fortunate. She drew the death card in the tarot deck and didn't know it was for her.

The BFH started on him again and it really bothered him. "Loser, loser, loser. Can't even handle one lousy woman and cried like a little bitch because you were so afraid. Loser, loser, loser, and who is this Dame Largesse you fixated on. Some kinda rock star or actress."

'You Bitches wouldn't understand medieval literature. Dame Largesse is a legend. A robust, vivid, vibrant women who went out in the country side and fed the peasants and gave them wine, chesses, meat and bread out of generosity. She rode a donkey. Now leave me the fuck alone. I've got to get Lurch to help me move the gypsy's body."

"Lurch? Do you mean to say you have a friend?"

"Lurch is this guy I know from school. Nursing school. We were not qualified in the human way to become nurses. Kind' gives one pause, doesn't it? Lurch always needs money and he helps me out. It's symbiosis which is a term you don't understand."

"We understand you pretty damn well. Loser, loser, loser". Shrill laughter and shrieks. "Perverted necrophiliac: you come when they die.

How fucking weird is that?" As Erasmus was about to blast them. Fate happened to him in the form of two bold, and rapacious Latina girls who descended on him.

He was stopped on the street by two Latina women, Lula and Salameh, of Dress Up the Town, a Fox station and they wanted to do a make-over on him.

"You're now on camera right now. We'll do a complete make-over, clothes, attitude. It's very Joy of life. We want to help you find new meaning and vitality in your life."

"I don't need a make-over. I'm very clean and I'm just fine with my life."

"Ahem",said Lula, the blond one, "Correct me if I'm wrong but are you not wearing a short, white polyester shirt and black cotton pants, and diddle me shoes with white socks? And you say you don't need a make-over. We're the Fashion Police and you're under arrest." And she broke out in raucous laughter. They both got him under the arms and dragged him down the street.

"What's your name, honey," said Salameh, the more restrained, dark haired one, "Is it Nestor or Lisle?" When she stopped talking he told her his name. "I rest my case.. Your new name is Raz, ya' get me. Darling, we're going to show you what real women want in a man."

"Yes," said the ebullient Lula, "We're going to show you how to get your game on."

"What makes you think I want to relate to the ladies? I'm kind of a lone wolf, said Raz. "I'm a taxidermist and can't wear good clothes to work."

"A taxidermist! How interesting. Working around all those lovely, dead things," said Lula. "My sentiments, exactly," said Raz. "I happen to like dead things. The dead never hurt anyone. It's the live people you've got to watch out for."

"A sensitive man and tortured soul. You don't know how compelling that is, my friend. You've been hurt," said Salemeh.

"Mamasita's for carnitas and Margaritas especiales. Are you in or not, Raz. This is the opportunity of a life time," said Lula.

Raz said, "Si, porque no". He was thinking in an offhand kind of way how Lula would look with a knife in her chest and what a fine pelt Salameh's hair would be to wear on his head after he scalped her. And the cameras caught all the dialogue. And a free meal is in itself quite enchanting, or so Raz was thinking. Both were alpha females and would put up one hell of a fight. That intrigued him. Not that he would really consider them beauties for his art work. It was also a turn on. No girls had ever made a fuss over him before, and he was genuinely flattered. In fact, he felt quite elated and he was glowing pink.

"Dios mio, Jefe, you are so transparent, Raz. Like a little child. I ask you a question and you just say anything without thinking. You've got to get your game-on if you want to capture the heart of a girl," said Lula.

Salemeh interjected, "You've got to have a little mystery about you, Raz. Think of Cathy in Wuthering Heights. Would she have gone for Heathcliff if he were not a tortured soul. You're just too normal." Raz laughed so hard he got the hiccups.

He replied that he never had time for "the babes" as he had to attend his sick mother who had recently passed on. He replied, "Mom gave me life. So I gave my life back to her and looked over her for fifteen years."

"Oh, Raz, you are so good. We are going to get you a girlfriend, truly. This is truly a human interest story par excellence. Your story is bigger than just a make-over. We'll need to get some footage of you at your job," said Lula with a toss of her honey colored hair. This caused a flutter in his cold, sick, reptilian heart and he thought "What if I skinned her and wore her hide." Then he grinned like a fox in the hen house.

Lula and Salemeh rained praise on him like a tsunami, and he went along with it. He never had it in his life Raz began to look on them as friends instead of prey. In his heart he knew he would never harm them. Friends were exempt…. Totally.

Raz sat back and watched Lula and Salemeh descend on their enchiladas like two hungry buzzards at a feast. He never saw two girls eat so much and with such gusto. They were fine representatives of the species, female, he decided. He noted the ambiance of the place with its red and white checkered table cloths, red candles, and antique walnut bar. It was peopled by young Latino couples in love, and there was a Mariachi band playing Cielito Lindo (My Pretty Little Heaven). Fresh red and yellow tulips graced each table and the food was fresh and well seasoned. Raz liked Mexican food and he more delicately devoured his food. The girls asked about his early years and he embroidered a tale of domestic bliss and maternal love and compassion instead of the real story. His mother was anything thing but warm and caring. So he described sitcom moms leaving out the names like the one on The Brady Bunch reruns which he watched growing up. The real truth was that Raz raised himself and did a bad job of it. Very early on he liked to watch things die. In the end he gave his mom the credit for making him a success. And it was true but she had made a monster. He was a feral child as if he was raised by wolves.

Chapter Five

Saturday in the first week of November Raz had his big make-over. It was decided that after the make-over, Lula and Salemeh would interview him at his place of work. He became like a little boy on Christmas morning. He was so excited he was stumbling over himself and he was fidgeting like a new bride. They noticed that Raz was still the little boy who sought maternal love and praise. So they gave this kind of love to him. It was instinctive on their parts and for once in his life he felt what love was really like and he would do anything to please them.

First, they went to the Ralph Lauren Salon where he got cruise wear such as navy blue dress Jackets and tasteful khaki pants and designer jeans. Also they got him tee shirts with the Polo logo and tasteful designer socks in any color but red. They introduced him to Florscheim shoes, Nike sneakers, and the beauty of tasseled loafers. They got him three pairs of five hundred cowboy boots. Armani suits were next and no man is complete without an Armani tuxedo.

The girls shouted encouragement at every turn like, "Hijole! Aint he the Bomb. Que Hombre!" or "Boy, you look good enough to eat." They also told him he looked so hot they were about to climax. This caused him to go pink and cackle. They finished the day with casual wear from Calvin Klein, and a visit to "His Parlance," a top of the line male hair salon, where he got a Mohawk cut. Lastly, to please Salemeh, he got a small diamond ear stud and the tattoo of a coiled cobra across his shoulders.

Salemeh and Lula, both shouted, "Merry Christmas, Raz. Now, you're a player!" and they did the hoochie dance around him. Raz was so overcome with gratitude, he burst into tears. Not one person in his life had ever been so kind and foolhardy as these girls. He was, after all, a bumbling serial killer and tigers cannot change their stripes. The camera caught it all but for his perverse, and tortured soul.

"Ay, this is an Ugly Duckling Story, que no?' chirped Lula. "From baggy boxers to Calvin Klein briefs. Quite a story, no? You happy, now, honey?"

"Let's get you out to greet your public. You're Big Time, now," interjected Salemeh."

And indeed, he was a "cool guy"" even though his face was not that of a pharaoh. Raz thought of the Mark Twain quote, "Clothes make the man. Naked people have little or no influence in the world." He remember the snooty clerk in Ralph Lauren who gave him the onceover and then shrugged. He would deal with her at some point. Irena from Bosnia, the anorexic.

He remembered DOM saying the doctor had to turn his back on her when he talked to her because Erasmus was so ugly. "Well what do you say now, oh, dead one?" he thought. She was quite proud of her lame witticism, She used to pass out every day except Sunday when she watched all the evangelists on television, and he used to lovingly tuck her in bed on the other days, He never doubted that the situation was normal and par for the course. He just thought that all adults were fucked up like Holden Caulfield in Catcher in the Rye. Raz knew quite a lot about literature and not a lot about life and people. And he really believed Lula and Salemeh had made him a new man. Raz was riding on the current of his newborn fame. His story had gone national and Udon's Taxidermy Shop was flooded with orders from all over the world so much that the owner, Don, moved to much larger quarters, and Raz got a six figure income. The final filming showed him working on a mountain lion and it boded well for Raz. The story was picked up by the national news media and Udon's Taxidermy shop became a national concern with Raz making a six figure salary. Luck Be a Lady Tonight.

Chapter Six

Like any wealthy man he wanted the things money could buy, a mansion in Chestnut Hill and a fire engine red Lamborghini. He added a lush suite for his mother all in shades of light gray and pastel pink, and he denied her nothing. He took one entire floor for his studio where he did his private projects that of turning people into mythical figures. It was kind of like Madame Tussaud's Wax Museum, only his creations were once alive. He considered that he was in the resurrection business and that he was immortalizing them. But because of his frailty he had a hard time getting his subjects, and more often than not ended fleeing the premises in danger of getting a beat down or worse. Such was the case with his gym instructor.

She, being a little gold digger, invited him out. She was just his type with long waist length, auburn hair and yellow cat eyes with a dancer's build, thin and elongated. He accepted her invitation for a home cooked meal, and came armed with a bottle of Cabernet Savignon and a box of costly chocolates. Seductively, she rolled a strawberry on her tongue and grabbed his flaccid cock. He removed her hand from his cock, saying, "All things in time, dearest."

Stung by her rejection she put on her kittenish pouty face for him. He laughed out loud and told her she resembled her Persian cat. True to form she asked if he wanted to eat pussy while holding her cream colored, Siamese cat.

"Yes," he replied, "but not in the way you might think."" He told her to give him her panties and he held them up to his nose.

She tiptoed over to him and told him to meet her upstairs, and she tongue kissed him.

He said, "Thanks for the scintillating conversation, You're not an English major, I trust."

"Phys Ed," she replied.

"Now why didn't I know that," he said

He followed the trail of rose petals up to her bed which was festooned with lacy pillows, and stuffed animals where she lay spread eagled like a rotten doll.

"Come and get it, tiger," she said.

"I feel like I'm in a porn movie."

She said, "Do whatever you want with me. I'm flexible."

"Do you like role playing, you filthy doll." And he went to strangle her with her own panties.

She threw him off her and reached in her bedside end table and brought out a pearl handled derringer, placing it on his forehead, and pulled the trigger. And she had a laugh riot. "I've got three slugs in the chamber. Want to get lucky again," she said.

Raz began to cry big, copious tears begging her not to kill him. And did she know she was his Degas Ballerina and that he would immortalize her for all time. She asked him who Degas was and he went into his Degas tutorial. And he knocked the gun from her hand but she recovered it.

"You want to kill me, slab me and stuff me like one of those animals you work on. What reason do I have not to off you. What you gonna' tell me that you're a nice guy? Tell you what you"re gonna clean my entire house, including the fridge & stove. Here's a scrub bush for the oven: get down on your hands and knees. And you're gonna mop and wax all my wood floors and vacuum my Persian rugs, ya cry baby. I have No respect for you. You aren't even strong enough to subdue me."

Raz did all the cleaning and developed a sore back and bruised knees as a result of it. She kept waving around the gun in his face and laughing uproariously.

"You know what you're going to have to pay me off and since you cleaned so well, I require your cleaning services weekly. If you don't like it, Frankly Madam I don't give a damn…"

By this time Raz had slowly backed out of the room and he made a break for the door amidst a hail of bullets. It was like one of those old television westerns in a saloon shoot out. This little misbegotten event cost Raz $100,000. He learned immortality was over-rated on the scale of things worth doing. And he learned Cleanliness was next to Godliness.

And speaking of Godliness, Mamie June required him to attend church functions and the Sunday services which took four hours of prayer and singing, He felt very close to God and Reverend Ponders took him on like a wayward son. At this time it was discovered Raz loved little children, especially the needy ones. He loved them not in a serial killer way. He actively played games with them like hide and seek, Monopoly, and cards. He was, in effect, a big kid himself. By mentoring and loving them he was healing himself. It was love he never had from his mother nor his absentee father. He took them to movies, sports games and amusement parks. Mamie June was delighted at his transformation.

He told her he loved her more than he loved his mother. Mamie June laughed in her big, sonorous way and said she had the Angel Gabriel sitting on her left shoulder. And as was her custom she prepared an after service repast and fed the hungry each Sunday at three PM. Anyone, child or adult, was welcome in her humble house. So Mamie June heaped his plate with country ham, grits, greens, macaroni and her special potato salad. She also baked cherry, and apple pies. Slowly Christian precepts crept into his psyche. He began to question his romance with Death. He began to approach the wayward mothers and buy their children, and being junkies, coke addicted mothers, they were all too eager to get rid of their children. The only stipulation Raz had was that they leave town. He then would give the children to Mamie June to raise. He bought a big Germantown mansion for Mamie and her charges and paid all expenses, food, mortgage and the like.

One day in church a little dark eyed boy came up to Raz and said, "Can you help me Mister Raz? I hate my mommy. She lets him stick it in me. I'm scared. He said he'd kill all of us if I told."

Raz asked him how long this had gone on and the boy said since he was six and he was nine now. And he was scared for his little sister, Suzie, age two, who was beginning to cry in her sleep. Raz got his address and name and promised to make it stop. And Thanatos was surging in his veins.

When in doubt, Raz went to DOM (dear old mom).

"You are sure changing, Hon," she replied. "From stuffing dead things to social worker."

"I don't need a soul synopsis, mommy. I need advice. Should I kill them or not? They're hurting innocent children. I told you the situation."

The BFH started again. "Psycho killer. Ed Gein's protégé. Loser, loser, loser. Euww, Ill. You never needed a reason to kill. before. Never. Never, Never." Their voices ricocheted in his head.

"Yes, I think you should kill them, Doll. It's fun being dead. A real gas. You get to know things you otherwise wouldn't know. For instance, the gypsy you killed and stuffed was a Santeria High Priestess, and she vows vengeance" said DOM.

"What can she do: she's dead like Marilyn Monroe. I mean, really dead."

"The hands of the dead extend into the world of the living. She will fell you in the moment of your greatest triumph which is yet to come. I think you better prepare for the worst. My hands are tied: I can't help you."

"Mommy, Is there any way you can convince her it was just good clean fun? That it's an honor to be chosen for my art menagerie?" Raz asked.

"Your idea of good clean fun is a tad perverse, darling boy," said DOM.

When you don't know what to do, do nothing. She's powerful evil, son. I cannot intervene: I'm powerless. I told her you were basically a good son except for that one main slip up, killing me."

"Oh, what a thing to deal with. My own eminent demise. It's kind of like being diagnosed with stage four cancer."

"Who said anything about death? There are many things worse than death," said DOM.

"Are you having a good time, mommy?" asked Raz.

"Of course, sonny boy. Just because I'm dead it doesn't mean I stop being a rotten bitch." DOM had a laugh riot.

Raz went into his studio to look at the gypsy and he saw her dead eyes were following him about the room. They were wrathful.

When he went to work all the dead beast's eyes came alive, and he felt really scared. This was not lost on the BFH.

"Oh poor thing. Poor thing. He's scared shitless. EUW, did you fuck her as she was dying or did you come in your pants? Why not fuck them and really enjoy yourself? You're entitled. Euw, ill, ill, ill."

They were screeching at him and he felt nauseous. He laid on the floor and screamed for an hour. Then he took a creature bath to replenish his failing strength. It worked, the sloshing around nude in their entrails. He then completed all his work and went home to fall into a soundless sleep. He dreamed of his dark god, Thanatos, a skeletal face with rheumy red eyes.

Raz began to stalk little Emile's parents so he could learn their routines and find a time when they were both home and Emile was not. The perfect day, was Wednesday, when Emile's father, Jorge Dragoon, was off from his trash collector Job, and his mother, Peachie, was off from her truck stop waitress position.

He upon approaching noted the overgrown weeds n their yard and the garbage cans full of empty bottles and beer cans. "Escapees from reality", he muttered to himself. He gained entre into the house with a set of fake IDs supplied by Lurch, his petty crime friend. His only friend. He noted her dancer's build, and athletic grace and thought, "Goldie Hawn except a harpy." She will be My Degas ballerina. Jorge with his robust build and ruddy complexion and curly black locks was an exact rendition of Bacchus and his 'pards. Bacchus was the Greek god of drink who also had a pair of leopards in tow at all times. The thrill of the kill was upon him and he glowed pink with exhilaration. He played the part of the concerned counselor well. He told them that Emile was disturbed and did not play with the other children. He further stated that Emile engaged in inappropriate sex play with the younger boys. Was he a bed wetter and did he light fires, he asked. His mother was quick to deny it all, saying Emile was just a little depressed and he was just naturally reserved and shy. Raz let them both rattle on about their happy home life, and Emile's sublime happiness and normalcy. He acted as though he thought they were the family out of "Leave it to Beaver". Then after they had exhausted themselves talking, he took out the gun and said, "I know what you both do to the boy: he told me. Say your prayers because you're going to die." She let loose an eerie scream like that of the little figure in Munch''s painting, "The Scream".

"Scream all you want. Nobody is their neighbor's keeper." Never a good marksman he first shot their fat Siamese cat and Jorge rushed him and got a shot in the belly for his bravado. He purposely saved Peachie for the last just to see her beg for her life. He said, "Relax, sweetheart. Death is easy and life's a bitch. Think how they'll miss you at the PTA meetings. I doubt you ever attended even one of them." The he plugged her in the heart.

Then he called Lurch to help him bag the pedophiles, and take them back to his studio in the mansion. It's times like this when one realizes the beauty of having one true lifelong friend.

Chapter Seven

Raz left the transport to Lurch giving him the keys to the front door and his secret studio. Then he cleaned up the mess thanking God in merciful Heaven that no neighbor's came to investigate and that the clean up was easy as they had wood floors not carpeting. Raz after cleaning went up the stairs to check on the two year old child who had slept through the whole fiasco and she held out her little fat arms to be held. He took her in his arms and whispered in her ear, "My baby you're going to have a very happy life." Then he made her food and heated up her milk bottle and played peekaboo and clap hands with her while waiting for Emile to return home from school.

He held Baby Suzie all day lavishing affection on her until she almost burst with happiness. He read Lewis Carroll's Alice through the Looking Glass and she cooed and put her little fat finger on the illustrations. Raz believed babies were far more intelligent than people knew. He talked regular English to her because he believed that babies talked "baby talk" because adults taught them to talk that way. He was certain Suzie was not a little dollop of cuteness: she was a curious, thinking being. Raz had a lot of "kid" still left in him because he never really had a childhood: he was always looking after his mother from early on.

When Emile arrived home he was glad to see Raz but puzzled as to where his parents were. Raz told them they had to go far away because of an emergency and that they would be staying with him in his great big house until his parents returned. Emile asked when they were coming back and Raz said maybe in a year and he saw a flicker of relief pass quickly over Emile's face and Raz smiled. This would be his chance to mentor them. He would teach them the classics and about all kinds of music and art. He would bring all the delights of the world to them.

It would be Raz's Palace of Pleasure he determined and later that day he with them in tow went to a bookstore and bought books on horses, dogs, cats and dinosaurs. He remembered these from his childhood days. Furthermore, he got The Tales of Narnia, Winnie The Pooh, and the Harry Potter books. Emile also added books to the heap of things like books on butterfies, American folk heroes, cowboys, and gangsters. Then they got loads of show and learn books for Suzie. He would have her reading in six months. He knew babies could learn. He researched this in his medical library. He also arranged for a nanny and a therapist for Emile. The nanny, a strapping black dynamo resembled Mamie June, tall and plump. The therapist resembled Woody Allen on a bad day.

He decided then to call it a day. The day had been very eventful to say the least and he had to report to DOM. He put the children, who both demanded that he read from Harry Potter which he did in his melodious contralto voice. He had also brewed up a pot of hot chocolate with marsh mellows for them.

Then he crept up the stairs to his mom's suites.

"Erasmus, you surprise me with this new fascination with children. You were never into kids before. You don't plan to stuff them, do you?" asked DOM.

"No, Mamie June got me into kids. I feel very close to them like they were my own. I just had no reason to socialize with them before. They are so fresh, innocent, and needy. They need me. And I need them. I won't have them be throw-away children. I might've turned out differently if I'd of had help."

"So, you're going to remake them with a happy childhood. So save them, save yourself symbolically," replied DOM.

"I do love them, mom. You're a sharp, ol' gal," he said.

"You sure you won't get any odd notions, Erasmas?"

"I go by Raz now, mom. And no, I'm sure. Should I introduce them to you?" he asked.

"You must never tell them I'm dead and am your mom," she said.

"Mr. Mojo say first born son introduce you as Madam Swan, circus performer with plastic face," said Raz.

"Raz, since when are you so funny?" she said

"Since always, mom. And the little birdies go tweet, tweet, tweet."

"Okay, Raz, but make sure the nanny doesn't know me. It would freak her out that I'm dead. This is all kinds of freaky."

"Some of the best folks are freaks, mom. So far I've got My Dame Largesse, My Degas Ballerina and my Bacchus and his 'pards. I need Regnoir's Lady in the Red Hat, Botticelli's Venus, Jesus and God, King Arthur and the Knights of the Round Table, and some dyads, and the god, Pan. I'll graft two goat legs onto a barrel chested man. I know the last one will be a real challenge."

"Son, you are one fry short of a happy meal," said DOM.

Chapter Eight

T he realm of Thanatos had Raz in its thrall. He led him into his studio that Saturday night and he lit some black candles for atmosphere. Instead of Black Sabbath he played Led Zapellin at concert level. "You need coolin'/ Baby I aint foolin" He lit some myhr incense and stripped naked, He avoided the gypsy's brutally angry stare. It was so fearsome it felt like acid eating into his skin and the eyes of all the dead seemed to follow him around the room. He was unnerved so he threw back a couple of shots of Ouzo which burned all the way down.

First, he removed the bullets from their carcasses. It was kind of like fishing for gold. Then he spread them on the table and looked lovingly into their dead eyes. He became aroused by the gash of Peachie's turgid clit. She was one of those women who had a nasty, jutting vagina, and the rot smell of it was overpowering. He mounted her and went in and out as he was able, shouting and groaning "Tell me you don't feel this, Bitch. You stupid cow. Feel, dammit, feel." Then he came up a storm, literally. Thunder crackled and rain splattered. And then the dead muscles contorted and tightened and he was stuck in the corpse… until morning.

The BFH had a laugh riot with this one. "Lookit, he's stuck like a square peg in a round hole. Damnation and perfidy.. Stuck inside a dead women. You just like to crack open a cold one. You like 'em dead and cold like an Edgar Allen Poe heroine. Now people will know how sick you are. They'll lock you away in the looney bin where you belong. Or maybe you'll fry for the murders. Ya think Jesus would like what you do and you call yourself a Christian. Your sordid little secret will be out. Yellow journalism to the max. Loser! Loser! Loser! Haaaaaaaa!" they screamed.

Imagine the nanny's surprise to walk by and see Mr. Raz in such a position. If she was horrified she never showed it. She said, "Hello Mr. Raz, I'll get the hot water and the Vaseline." She acted like it was the most common thing in the world. When his penis came out all raw and red, she coated it with Vaseline giving it a little goodbye pat as she walked away humming an old spiritual tune, "Nobody Knows the Trouble I've Seen…"

She was the model of decorum as she served the bran muffins, coffee and orange juice. After that Raz made sure he didn't go "frigid air". Yet, the noir doesn't end there. Raz often ate parts of their hearts while listening to Janis Joplin's 'Little Piece of My Heart." He calmly put a thousand dollar bill on the counter where she was working which she quickly snatched up and put it into her bra, and without further ado she continued her domestic duties. Raz was well pleased by het stoic manner and he told her about his mother and entrusted her with care of DOM whose clothes needed to be changed periodically. He didn't confess to murder as that would be counter productive. Some things just exceed the realm of polite conversation. So Raz went back into his secret studio while Esmeralda, the nanny, tended the children preparing them for their day.

While skinning them he broke into song, "The Hills Are Alive with the Sound of Music." And he salted their hydes to dry out their skins. And he put on Jorge's skin and danced around the room until fatigue got the best of him. He had to sleep before he went into work that night. He had fitful dreams of the gypsy who came for her "pound of flesh" and she ripped his heart out of his chest, holding it up like a sodden trophy singing gypsy incantations. He awoke to strange, otherworldly music. Esmeralda was playing Haitian music for the children. He felt afraid for them. It was clearly voodoo music or so he thought. He ordered Esmeralda to never play that kind of music again and he left on a cloud of unease.

Destiny. That which we cannot foresee or control. Destiny, the trickster. That night Philamena Pfumph walked into Raz's life, the only girl he did not want to stuff. She was his new taxidermy assistant, newly hired by Don Udon. She was a thin like branches in winter and six feet tall. Her long platinum hair shined with celestial elegance and grew down to her ass. She had an odd heart shaped face and large azure colored eyes, full of pain. Looking into her eyes was like being bathed in the cooling rain. Her pale skin had a slight bluish tint like skimmed milk, and she wore absolutely no make-up. She wore an R. Crumb tee shirt with stretch jeans

which cleaved to elegant form. She wore a red Philly's cap backwards with her hair in a pony tail secured by colored rubber bands. She seemed to be at ease with the dead things, and was very deft with her hands and wordlessly she anticipated his every need. She was very like a doe, soft and reclusive, speaking only when spoken to. He felt rather than heard her and intuited a wall of pain within her. From that moment Raz moved his soul next to hers, subtle and in obtrusive, he was. He used what he thought was a good pick-up line.

"So, Philamena, what do you think of that guy, Nietche," he queried. She paused, startled like a deer in the headlights, and replied, "I think he's an ass bite."

Raz broke out in cackles and proclaimed it an apt summation. "Sometimes I think I'm the Super Man, Philamena."

"Then you're an ass bite, too. Nietche is what's wrong with this world. Everybody out for his own ass. Where's the love? The only men I attract are heartless bastards."

"Who says I'm attracted?" said Raz.

"Well you are, aren't you," she countered.

"You're not my type," replied Raz.

"What's your type?" she asked.

"Beautiful, trashy, and cold to the touch," he said.

"So, I'm guessing now. You like the Undead," she said.

"In a stretch, you could say so," he said.

"Then you'd love me. I'm frigid and I've faked it all my life," she uttered.

"And I'm impotent. We're just two wannabes," he said and laughed.

"I'm like making it with a dead woman, and a stage actress. Necro Numb," she said.

"Very witty. I like the consonance. You, a poet?" he asked.

"I'm a noir poet, of tainted love," she said. "So you're a necro vampire. I went out with this guy who tried to cut my neck and suck my blood. He was so good looking. Now he sings soprano."

"So, he's a Castrati, now?"

"No. but he may as well be," she said. "I have nine brothers. I grew up learning how to fight like a man. My parents, dyed in the wool

Catholics, never should have had kids. My mom was cold and depressed and dad was too warm, if you get me… Don't think because we had this little heart to heart, I'll go out with you..."

"I'm presuming nothing, Philamena. Hon, I'm impotent. Women make me very, very angry."

"Well, hot damn, I wouldn't have to fake it. We're made for each other," she said.

"Clearly, so," said Raz. "About the death thing, I hope you're not afraid…"

"Afraid of your puny ass. Not hardly," she said and hauled off and decked him.

When he came to with his head in her lap his heart was singing, "Philamena".

When he went to sleep in the early morning hour of 3:00 AM he dreamed of Philamena on pink sands with the roiling emerald waters caressing her blue white skin. She appeared as a nude mermaid brutally bound fishermen's nets and at first he thought her dead. He leaned down and kissed her on the lips and she moaned and opened her azure eyes. She spoke in a strange, otherworldly voice like this hiss of the ocean waters. He platinum hair was covered in seaweed, and was fanned out on the pink sand. He noted her small, innocent breasts with purple rose colored nipples and he felt a powerful urge to enter her slit which he did. And she rocked him like a ravaging succubus. She drained him of his manhood and he realized he had to set her free so he cut away the net and carried her back into the churning waters. Just a strand of her beauteous hair in his hand was all he had left of her. Sadness descended as he awakened with the taste of her on his lips. He noted the smell of the ocean lingered in the still air.

The next morning he decided Philamena should meet DOM, or "Madam Swan" as she had named herself. He told her the fake story of his love for a gifted fortune teller who had been very important in his life and how he had embalmed her and preserved her for all time. He claimed she had rescued him from a troubled youth as the gang leader of the murderous "Cue Balls."

Philamena took it all in with aplomb and glorious grace and remarked how alive she seemedand how pleased she was to "meet" her.

Chapter Nine

He realized he had to talk to DOM for advice. He went into her studio and received a riotous welcome.

"Sonny, boy, what's wrong? Ya look like you lost your best friend if you had one. I notice the bodies are piling up in your studio. I hear heavy footsteps on the stairs and then this absolute ghoul brings in two very large hefty bags and places them in your studio."

"That was my Degas Ballerina and Bacchus and his 'pards. I found just the right models for this piece of art. They're Emil's parents and you're never to tell him. They were pedophiles. Er, Double Plus Ungood, to quote Anthony Burgess," he said.

"So what is it? Has that Nanny, Esmeralda, found out what you're about. I know she comes in here to spritz me up every day. What else does she know," she said.

"I told her you were Madam Swan, a fortune teller, who died of cancer and wanted to be immortalized. Basically, she knows about my sexual proclivities. She found me in an compromising position: I got stuck on a girl, you might say," he said.

"She caught you in the act of cracking open a cold one? Oh, heavenly fuck. You're headed for jail," said DOM.

"She's a Haitian voodoo women. I make it worth her while to keep quiet. And it's Raz, now, mommy," he said.

"When, do I get to see my grandchildren, Erasmus?

"When, they've been here awhile. Another coupla' months, mom. I think I'm in love with this girl at work, Philamena," said Raz.

"In love? What're you trying to do, give me a heart attack? Was it that girl, Philamena you introduced me to?" she queried. "Give mommy a smoochie, dear."

He did and she slipped him some tongue and groped him. "If it doesn't work out there's always

Dear Old Mom as you call me, DOM."

"Mom, that is so outre. We can't just keep it in the family. It's just too weird for me," he said.

"Oh, now he's worried about weird. It's pretty weird, this stab 'em, slab 'em and stuff 'em."

"This girl, I want to marry her, and I never once imagined wearing her skin or her head on a plaque," he said.

"This is the start of a beautiful relationship," said DOM sarcastically. "Do you have any idea of how sexual I am now that I'm dead?"

"Don't be so sarcastic, mommy. And I prefer not to think about your sexuality," he said.

"Well, when does Madam Swan meet Cinderella again?" she asked.

"Well, after a while, I think. Do you know you look like a Dianne Arbus photo?" he asked.

"I do not look my age and I do not look like whoos-it either. I am a beautiful woman and you're a damn fool. You reject me and like the movie, Misery, I'm your number one fan," she said.

"What we have here is a problem. A quagmire," he said.

It's more a conundrum than anything else, I think," said DOM.

"You know I love you, mommy," he said.

"I know, dear," she said.

Raz, left his mother's studio in a state of worry. He was afraid Philamena would find out his true nature and reject him forever. The BFH, of course, would not let him off easily. They always attacked when he was weakest. And he was sick in heart so they revved up to add fuel to the fire, so to speak..

"So, Raz, said the BHF, "How do you plan to keep it from her? You'll have to invite her over at some point in time. She knows you're an artiste and you can't hide Love's Labor Lost, forever. And DOM still wants to jump your bones: she's really got the hots for you. Euw, Ill, ill, ill. It's so gross we could just go hurl. Philamena is on her way over right this minute, bringing chocolate croissants and a box of Nigerian coffee. You know she'll want to see your etchings, so to speak. What will be your excuse not to show her and will you take her to church with you as well? It's Sunday morning and you always go. She'll get to meet Blackie. Oh, is that politically incorrect? Mamie June and what if Mamie slips up and tells her you're a sicko, a perv, and a murderer. Euw, Ill, ill, ill."

I'll tell her I'm not ready to show her my work or better yet, I'll show her my bird collection from when I was a boy. So there. I solved the problem, Bitches, and besides I already introduced her to mommy. She thinks she's Madam Swan, a fortune teller. So what have you got to say now. Also, I can pass it off as sculpture, pure art," Raz said to the wind.

"How you gonna' explain that you use real human skin on your sculptures, motherfucker?"

I"ll just say it's a polymer and plastic mix, my own secret remedy. What did you expect me to 'fess up? Nunca pasa and that's what I'll tell the press at the Met when I show my work."

"Oh, hubris. Who said you were good enough for the Metropolitan Museum of Art?" said BFH.

"Oh, I'm good enough. What you Bitches know about high art could be transcribed on the head of a needle," he said. "This conversation is over, go fuck yourselves."

"Oh, the vanity. The extreme hubris. Don't get too exalted. You'll get caught. The Gypsy has something in store for you. Vengeance, and we know what it is but we'll never ever tell you. We're not your friends. Be careful for what you wish for: you might just get it. Yes, we can see into the future," said the BFH.

With false bravado, Raz insulted them calling them, "Vampiric Harpies," and "slutty whores who drank a mile of come." Yet, he was anything but self assured and they knew it. They shrieked with laughter and Raz flushed pink with fear and rage. He ran down the stairs to answer the door bell but not before locking his studio door and the door leading to DOM's suites.

It was early December and Philamena Pfhumpf was pounding on his door and ringing the door bell repeatedly. She was dressed as a Christmas elf with a forest green leotard, red and white striped stockings, kickie boots and a white rabbit fur hat. She wore pigtails intertwined with holly berries and on her face and hair she had sprinkled green and gold glitter. She sang all the lyrics to "We Wish You a Merry Christmas" and her voice had an oboe sound to it, low and melodic.

The she very forcefully demanded to know what time it was and both times he answered 6:00 AM. And she acted affronted. Finally she yelled. "It's Christmas time, ya idiot!!", and abruptly barged right past him into the foyer like the tomboy she was. She handed him a large basket full of various cheeses, chocolate croissants, and a number of different fruits like bananas and strawberries. She had two giant silver tureens, one being hot chocolate, and the other was hot Nigerian coffee. Raz caught her up in his arms and gave her a big kiss. It was December 10th.

The children came timorously down the stairs followed by Esmeralda, their nanny, and Raz introduced her as a friend from work. And she went over to the children and kissed them lightly on the tops of their heads and they were awash in the strong scent of roses (Tea Rose Perfume). Esmeralda, knowing her place, began to serve up the goodies, and arrange a cheese platter. Philamena first put Lou Rawls' CD on the CD player, "It's Christmas time, Pretty Baby, and the snow is fallin' down." She also had Lena Horne, the Temps, Dianna Ross and Bing Crosby CDs. Boris Karloff reciting the story of The Grinch was a big hit with the children. Slowly the children warmed up to Philamena and soon they were all over her lap and full of hugs and kisses.

"You sure make the case for Dame Largesse out of Medieval literature," said Raz.

"That's the greatest compliment anyone ever gave me," she said and the voice rose up like champagne bubbles. And she retorted that she had special gifts for each child. There was a Lionel Train set for Emile and Malibu Barbie for Suzie.

"There is nothing more intriguing then knights, ladies and monsters," said Raz.

I'm one of the monsters."

"I always like the monster's best," said Philamena. "Fire breathing dragons are more compelling than Lords, knights and kings." And Raz blushed pink and got an erection. "Lady Philamena, I do thee wed," said Raz.

Philamena was intrigued and delighted by the sudden declaration, and said it was a bit too soon to know whether it could happen. Raz replied that he knew all he needed to know and would she say yes. The sound of her happy laughter was like a hundred tiny bells all ringing at once. And Raz said he would give her time to consider it but the offer was on the table.

Philamena said she would go with them to get a tree and some greenery for the fireplace. Before that, she helped Emile set up his train set on the perimeters of the living room. They laid all the tracks and had it running after one and a half hours. Esmeralda weighed in for Raz, saying, "Lady, I advise you to say yes. Mr. Raz is a very wealthy man and a rich man is as easy to love as a poor man and he is a great artist. You would want for nothing."

Philamena was savvy and no stranger to poverty and reasoned that the best way to learn about a man was through his children. She found out that there was a troubled background with the children's real parents, the Dragoons, and that the family had abandoned them.

She learned that Raz was kind to them and very responsive to their needs. And he was an even tempered disciplinarian and never deviated from the house rules so as to give them comfort and certainty. She learned from snatches of conversation that Emile had been sexually abused by his father and that the mother failed to protect him. Raz just sat back and let Philamena work her magic. He let her run the show and he knew that she, as well, had been abused by her father. They adored her and were all over her with touches and kisses. She glowed with a kind of silver light like that of sun light through winter icicles and he knew she was "the one".

They went out into the overcast snowy day to get the biggest tree possible and ended up with a thirty foot high Silver Spruce tree. Suzie became agitated when they didn't chose a little tree, so Raz bought it for her and put it in her room. Then they all gathered around the main tree to decorate it. They used colored Italian lights, bubble ornaments, and little red robin toys from Raz's bird collection. Philamena saw the true artist in Raz that day as his little dead birds throbbed with preternatural life. He was a very gifted man. Philamena and Suzie worked alone on Suzie's little tree with white Italian lights and little, soft white angels, and silver Christmas tree balls. It was like a girls' night out.

Raz prepared a large clam and oil pasta dish with fried eggplant, and an immense and colorful salad, while Esmeralda baked honey wheat bread and apple and cherry pies.

They had Cabernet Savignon for the adults and Almond milk for the children. Phillamena baked her only specialty, lemon chicken with

Portobello mushrooms. Philamena usually ate a Vegan diet of grains and nuts. When everyone else had gone to bed, Raz and Philamena sat by a smoldering fire, in silence, watching the snow storm outside falling, falling falling…Each of them knew that love could be destroyed by the tumult of words. From that moment on, Philamena became the writing on his heart. He was never without her soft, ebullient presence.

Chapter Ten

Yet in spite of his powerful love for Philamena and the children, Thanatos was a hard master who demanded tribute. Raz continued his nightly ramblings for prey amongst the homeless for they would not be missed. He found his "God" amidst them who resembled Charlton Heston on a bad day. He had a magnificent presence and a powerful face. His hair was long and silver like sunlight from behind a cloud. His blue eyes crackled with what seemed to be arcane knowledge. He looked liked a wise man, a philosopher king, a man among men. Raz awaited some grand pronouncement, some key to the meaning of life and the universe. The man merely pondered Raz for a time as if he were going to say something fortuitous and he said, "I like hot dogs."

Then Lurch chloroformed him and lifted his body into his white van. Those were the last words the man said and Raz felt grandly disappointed. He felt it to be a personal affront to him.

"Lurch", he said on the way back, "He looked like he was going to say something really profound, like why are we here, and he comes out with the hotdog bit, I feel cheated."

Lurch, who looked like the vampire out of the film, "Nosferatu", merely grunted in assent. In all of Raz''s assignations, Lurch was there as Raz was too puny to waylay them and then transport the bodies to his studio. He was Renfield to Raz's Dracula. From his bony, bald skull to his black jack boots he screamed "monster". He was a bottom feeder in the criminal hierarchy, a $500 hit man, a raper of grandma's, a petty thief of East Indian corner stores, and an over-all scoundrel. He welcomed Raz's jobs like manna from heaven, so to speak and they were The Ghastly Duo. Both loved dead women and worshipped at the Altar of Thanatos. Lurch was somewhat dim due to his constant use of illicit drugs. He was not brilliant enough to rob banks or pull off jewel heists. He had a nefarious hobby as well. Lurch went to stranger's funerals and he regaled the other mourners with lewd, lascivious exploits involving him and the dearly departed. When the people realized he was a pervert they expelled him from their ceremony. He then coarsely suggested that they suck his dick or something similar. Then as a parting shot from Dicken's Christmas Carol, he recited Tiny Tim's, 'God Bless Us All, Each and Everyone." Not what Dickens intended.

Lurch accompanied Raz into his studio, deposited the body and asked to keep Raz company as he worked. Raz inculcated him with the practice of bathing in the entrails of the deceased and he loved it. Then Raz allowed him to walk around in the skin of "God" while playing various show tunes like Westside Story (When you're a jet you're a jet all the way). Raz sang along as he knew all the lyrics by heart. Raz became quite jocular and eager to have a participant in his strange rituals. When Raz served up the heart of the man, he played Janis Joplin's "Little Piece of My Heart." The irony was lost on Lurch who called Janis, a "lezzie bitch".

Then Lurch, swilling Green Chartreuse, confessed to sleeping with Jackie, Raz"s mom.

Raz grimaced and then roared with laughter. "Then I guess that makes you a Motherfucker, too."

"Too? You mean you did your own mother, Raz? That aint even Kosher."

"It only happened once," explained Raz.

"Oh, only once. That's okay, right. I'd hurl before I ever did my own mother," Lurch intoned.

"So would I. You got your good looks from your mom. Not. She looks like an Appalachian moonshiner and she has a moustache."

"Listen, faggot. Shut up before I pound ya' into very fine powder."

"I apologize, Lurch. Listen to me. Do you really think I can make him int

"Of course. Lookit' what you did with your own mom. Turned a sow's ear into a silk purse. She's got ass for miles and those tits... I tell you...."

'Listen, Lurch. My mother's sexuality is not something I even want to talk about. Can I turn that old bum into God. I'm afraid I can't do it.

"You can do it. You hand make the forms yourself. You are a skilled sculptor. You, the Man."

"Yeah, I AM the man. You're right," said Raz. "I think I'll turn him into Yahwek, the Old Testament God. We're done here: get cleaned up and burn your clothes when you get home.

No evidence, my friend."

So Lurch cleaned up and left Raz alone.

Chapter Eleven

After a night of ghoulish endeavor, Raz's thoughts turned gently toward Philamena, and he decided he had to be next to her warm and loving spirit. Then he hit on a brilliant idea. Why not have a Kid's Day Out. Why not create the ideal childhood experience, a normal childhood, something neither one of them had experienced. He started by going to The Owlish Unicorn, a specialty shop with odd and witty items. He bought two Doctor Denton Pajamas, (the ones with feet built into them). His was baby blue: hers was pastel pink. He got her some bunny ears and a jester's hat for himself. Then he bought children's books like Alice Through the Looking Glass, Winnie the Pooh, and the Tales of Narnia. For good measure, he also bought the Harry Potter series. He stopped by Bread Prophet, a creative bakery store, and ordered cakes made in the shape of stars with pink and green butter icing. He also bought a number of Christmas cookies. Then he bought exotic juices like mango and papaya, and also the makings of hot chocolate and marsh mellows.

This being done, he showed up at her door and she was still wiping the sleep out of her eyes. He explained that they were both nine years old and "the grown-ups" were out. She loved the idea and caught on right away by saying her name was "Phil" and he was to be called, "Razberry."

"Do you like my hair Razberry? I washed it in pumpkin shampoo," she said.

"I think you are very pretty for a girl and I want to brush your shiny hair. Here get into these PJs, I'm gonna' give you pigtails. See all the pretty ribbons I bought you," he said. And she burst into giggles and they both donned their outfits changing in front of each other like innocent children. She came back with a silver engraved hairbrush and sat down on the couch letting him play with her hair. He tied one pigtail with a forest green ribbon, and the other with a red ribbon and she dumped gold and silver glitter on both of them and the echo of her laughter thrilled his jaded and perverse heart. The glitter made her even more otherworldly like a Christmas faerie. He drank in her beauty like fine aged wine and he knew she was "the one".

They adjourned to the kitchen to make a luscious pot of hot chocolate in a sterling silver tureen. The hot chocolate was made with a bitter sweet baker's brand and she put a cinnamon stick in each cup and floated the top with huge marsh mellows. And they cut into the star cakes and they tasted the various liqueurs used in the making of the cakes, Sambuca and Kahlua. Then they went back to her lush, comfortable living room. It was painted Marigold yellow and this was in stark contrast to a red overstuffed couch. The Walnut end tables had falcon's claws on them, and the effect was like that of sitting in a Parisian, country café. Impressionist posters graced her walls and even the white tiled bathroom had Marie Cassatt renderings of mother and child.

"Let's talk about the grown-ups," said Raz, "and I'll go first."

"Don't wanna," pouted Philamena.

"You're an old sourpuss, and what I say goes 'cuz I'm the boss not you. My daddy is real tall and good looking and mom bakes a lot and sews. She's not fat and ugly, no way. I got this little brother, and he's a real pain in the ass. I call him the Beaver. It's just that he's always confused about everything. My family's always going on picnics and stuff. My family is just swell. Mommy stays home to take care of me and the Beav."

"Okay, Razberry. My daddy's name is Rhett and he's super good lookin' and mommy is called Scarlet and we live in a big mansion in the South. Daddy says she loves the mirror more than us. Daddy bought me a nice pony and mommy is super mad. Daddy really loves me, and he would never ever hurt me. He says I am his little doll baby and he will do anything to make me safe and happy."

Philamena bent double and screamed, and the tears flowed. Raz knew just what to do: when one lances a boil the puss flows. He took her in his arms and let her scream and cry and curse. Only when she stopped trembling did he release her. He gently looked into her eyes, and sang, "Nobody Knows the Trouble I've Seen." She laughed out loud and admonished him to not quit his day job.

"I know what," she said, "the grown-ups are not here. Let's go jump on the bed and have a pillow fight. You won't tell on me, will you?"

"Scout's Honor and may witches boil me in hot oil if I do. Last one up is a rotten egg," he said and he got the jump on her and beat her up the stairs. He hid behind the door and walloped her with a huge pillow. They continued until they were out of breath. They both collapsed on the huge bed and then they got into the spooning position with Philamena in Raz's arms, back side to him. He got an instant erection and she knew it but she knew not to react.

He sighed, and said, "Not, yet, Phil, I'm only nine years old…but sometime in the foreseeable future. Phil, be my Maid Marion, my Lady Guinevere, right out of Arthurian Legend and I am the Dragon to love and protect you. You said you liked the monsters better than the kings and knights. I haven't forgotten what you said. Am I your man, Phil. Two broken halves make a whole."

"You be my man, Razberry. When in doubt take out the black woman in me. Yes, the answer is a resounding, yes, Razberry. My man, like a poem on my tongue. Sweet Seduction, Salacious.

I'm going to get a lot of poems out of you, darling. Will you look at the way the light's coming in yon window. It's just beautiful."

"You are the one that's beautiful, Phil. I love the waif in you and the powerful woman in you as well. If you ever need anything at all, say it once and you'll have it," he said.

"Let's take a nap together. I love when you say you'll protect me, Razberry," she said.

Like two coalescing waves they intertwined and fell into happy dreams that blotted out the world and its machinations. Raz dreamed of candy canes with arms and legs dancing like the Rockettes and Philamena dreamed she was in a deep, dark forest and Raz was the dragoon who came to lead her out of the gloom.

Philamena was beautiful in sleep like a Renaissance angel. There was a peace and contentment that came to Raz as he lay next to her that he never experienced before. He thought it would be fun to surprise her so he painted her toenails black while she slept. It was a small weird thing that would stay in her mind for a long time. And he knew it. To wake her up he trailed a garden rose over her face which she tried to bat away in her sleep. So he tongued kissed her and she finally awoke. She would not know about the toe nail trick until he was gone as he had put the Doctor Denton's Pajamas back on her sleeping body before he woke her. He had a hard-on and she laughed and punched him in the belly saying, "Oh, lookie

Peter's awake too. I'll show you mine if you show me yours." So they removed their pajamas and softly explored each other's body in the way little children do. Then, she burst out laughing when she saw her feet, and for revenge she began to tickle him and he laughed and tickled her back. This began another pillow fight and Raz had the upper hand this time. Then they took a bubble bath together and washed each other's body and Raz came in her hand. Philamena did not use any words of surprise or encouragement: she merely smiled her wondrous smile, and cleaned him up. They got back in their pajamas and later feasted on a Vegan vegetable and tofu meal. Philamena ate like a hunger ravaged beast and Raz thought, "It's always the skinny girls who eat the most." He knew he would keep surprising her each time. Perhaps, he would dye her pussy hairs pink someday…

After some pondering Raz decided that it would be good and well for him to further acquaint Philamena with his mother who assumed the identity of gypsy Madam Swan. She even wore scarves and large hoop earrings and a purple velveteen flounced skirt with a white peasant blouse and a short black leather vest. DOM really did a Spanish accent well and she was sure she had Philamena fooled. He phoned his mom and told her to get with the gypsy wear and the tarot cards. His mom was a vision in purple, gold and red and huge hoop earrings and she smelled of lilacs and pine incense. Though she did not move her body she could with great effort put expressions on her face which is no mean trick if you're dead.

Raz knew he had some explaining to do. 'Listen, Phil, I'd like you to see Madam Swan again. You know Dante's Seven Levels of Hell? Well, there are also levels of death. There's Dead as a Doornail dead, and there's Marilyn Monroe dead where you don't really die as you are suspended in a death like state and not completely dead. Powerful people are this kind of dead. There is a portal dividing the Living from the Dead and it happens to be behind my couch. And they can use telepathy to communicate with living people. Well, Madam Swan is number two dead. I can speak to her with my mind as I am an empath."

"You know, Raz, I think maybe your elevator doesn't go all the way to the top floor or maybe you're one fry short of a happy meal," said Philamena.

"I thought you'd say something like that. It's not Twilight Zone, Doll. It's real and I can prove it. Maybe you'll be able to talk to her. I just want the two of you to be friends. You're both very important to me," said Raz.

"Alrighty then, I'll take the bait. You've awakened my curiosity," said Philamena.

"You've made me a happy man," said Raz.

"That was my intent, darling," said Philamena.

They arrived as the sun was falling from the sky and the giant Squid would release its ink on the sleeping town. DOM had Esmeralda set up white candles in her studio everywhere, The scent of lilac permeated the tepid air. She put on folk songs from the sixties like Simon and Garfunkle, Bod Dylan and Judy Collins. The flickering candle light clearly showed the ravages of time, and her spiritual putrefaction. This made DOM look like Bride of Chuckie: this was something she didn't realize. She was so vain.

Raz let them in and they proceeded up the winding staircase to DOM's domicile and it never ceased to amaze Raz at his mother's capacity for the dramatic. She was stunning in her offbeat sort of way kind of like the movie, "Whatever happened to Baby Jane". She was Bette Davis incarnate. They made polite chit chat, "Ah, so you're a taxidermist, too, Dear," she purred. "How nice for you, Erasmus: you have a partner in crime, so to speak."

"Yeah, Mom. You nailed it. She's a real talent and, on the other hand, she's a noir poet," said Raz.

"So, do I hear wedding bells?" DOM asked.

"Mom, don't go there! We're waiting for the right time to take the final step," intoned Raz.

"The final step. Sounds like Death: are either of you, terminal?" Dom let out a raucous laugh.

Aw, Mom, you are embarrassing me," said Raz. "The first time I met her I asked her."

"You mean you turned my son down? You could do a lot worse. Rich, not bad looking and definitely not a rapscallion. He wouldn't be unfaithful like other men. I know my boy."

"Excuse me, Madam, are you his mother?" asked Philamena.

"No, not biologically, but yes, in spirit, I am. He likes to call me, Mom."

"I am considering marriage, Madam," she said and Raz blushed pink and was embarrassed to have an erection.

"Call, me Jackie, Dear. We don't stand on ceremony here," said DOM.

"Are you serious. Philamena?" asked Raz.

"Serious as a club foot Mohican," she laughed and kissed him fully on the mouth.

"Oh, hell, yes. Does a bear shit in the woods, is a blue jay blue, and is the Pope Catholic?" said Raz.

And that is how Raz became engaged like any regular guy. Thanatos always waited in the sidelines for his best protégé Raz. And Raz got her a ring so big that she had a hard time in raising her hand.

But Destiny, Wicked Lass, was not done with Ras yet. No. not by a long shot. Later that same day Etta June Bixby payed Raz a visit: she was his Botticelli's Venus. And she meant business. At first, Raz thought she was there to expose him or collect a large sum of his money. He began weeping right away, saying how "sorry" he was and such an honorable and honest life he was leading at that time and how his episode with her was his last.

She had a laugh riot, and Raz laughed along with her as she had a 38 aimed at his head: it was a nervous laugh. Etta explained that she required him to help frame her philandering husband with murder, her murder. She was diagnosed with stage four breast cancer and he was out every night playing hearts with a high fashion model named Antigone Thrushmore and not even trying to conceal the affair. In fact he even flaunted it saying when she was dead he'd have all her "lovely" money to do with as he pleased. He was a lustful Lothario and a callous cad. She also required that he stuff her and transform her into "Venus" on the Half Shell. She was the spitting image of Botticelli's Venus, with a long, lithe body with two pert breasts and a Renaissance face. She had him record her and she requested that he record her fears and hand wrote a note expressing the same. They went back to her palatial estate two hours before her husband was scheduled to come back and he said this would not be complete without a final dinner and he was a Cordon Bleu chef and what be her pleasure. She replied Coq Au Vin, asparagus spears, scalloped new potatoes, avocados. and Cherries Jubilee. She required Cabernet Savignon and a chaser of Remy as she wanted to "feel no pain". He shopped, came back and found her crying which was not surprising considering the circumstances. He sat beside her and put her head on his shoulder and gently wiped away her tears. He knew better than give her platitudes: she was too sharp for that. She gave him a packet of letters to give to her loved ones with the exception of her husband. She gave him the cold winter wind. She she indicated she gave him the word and he said, "This will be brief: you will not suffer. I promise you with all my heart. You will be the most beautiful Botticelli's Venus ever, the prize of my collection."

And Raz with gloves shot her in the heart and then buried the gun with her husband's prints on it under the little cupid peeing into the fountain in the front of the house. Naturally Raz was acutely aroused and came in his pants. The police found the gun and her affects (body) and all her money was left to Raz, her "dear friend". Need I say closed casket service, and tearful reminiscences by Raz and her friends and family. "She's in a better place now"…."such a dear girl taken in her prime." As for her body she had willed it to Raz to do as he saw fit in them interest of science. The last words she whispered, were "immortality".

He upon receiving the body skinned the body with flushing tools and salted the hyde and disposed of the body waste but not before bathing in her "effects". He was feeling quite jocular and said to no one in particular, "What's a ghoul like you doing in a situation like this?" And he had a laugh riot he poured an entire bottle of Shalimar into the gruesome mixture to honor her brave, noble personage. He sang a tribute tune especially to her. "I'm strictly a female female, all dressed up in ribbons and lace, and I pity any girl who isn't me tonight." And he ate her ass literally and found it delicious. In rendering the final project he was true to her flesh tones, a pinkish white, and he duplicated the Venus's long, languid body and graceful carriage of the neck. He added light brown hair tresses to obscure the genital area. She was perfection which was not supposed to exist on earth.

His next subjects were the dyads and the god Pan.

Chapter Twelve

When Raz came out of his studio at six am, he found little Emile sitting on the stairs waiting for him. He asked if his parents were coming back to get him and Suzie. Raz paused and said no. Relief showed on Emile's face. And Raz picked him an held him close and Emile asked if they were dead and Raz told him they died in a car wreck.

"Why did Daddy do those things to me? Why did Mommy let him?" he asked.

"Some people are just evil, Emile." said Raz. "Your Mother was afraid of him, too and feared he'd leave her if she interfered. There is no real reason for evil, Emile. It just is. People are both good and evil, too. Your parents loved you, Emile, but they failed you."

"I hate Daddy for what he did to me and I hate Mommy more."

"You love them, too. Emile. I know you do, my sweet boy. It's gonna' take a long time but you're gonna' be okay. Just talk to the lady. And why don't I read Harry Potter to you so you'll go back to sleep?" And he kissed Emile on the top of his head.

"You know nothing like that will ever happen to either of you here. You're completely safe and then when Philamena marries me we'll be a family." And he gently patted Emile on the head. The boy sighed and smiled with relief. He was soon asleep.

Then the BFH decided to spoil his happiness as they were wont to do. '' So, it's Raz, happy family man. How long before you kill them. Once a perve, always a perve. What excuse do you give her that you can't get it up? Sorry, Darling, you're not dead."

"I will never harm them. And I do get erections around Philamena," he replied.

"You cannot deny your true nature. You're a killer," said BFH.

"I am an artiste. I Immortalize them with my skills," he said. "The killing is incidental. I hate to interrupt your soul fest but I've got to sleep: I've just completed my Venus."

The BFH were rarely dismissed and used to torturing Raz until he broke. "You'll never get away with it. The gypsy has sworn vengeance. Just wait until you scale the heights: then she'll topple you. She has powerful Santeria magic."

"Á dead woman can hurt me? I don't think so. Tell me some more grim Faerie Tales."

"She is dead, but not dead. Her spirit lives and she is very dangerous. Ever notice how the animal's eyes follow you in your work shop. She has awakened their spirits."

The BFH beat him down to the sound of raucous laughter. Raz went to bed awash in a cold sweat and he saw her angry, wrathful eyes staring at his heart as if to rip it out. She was the one statue he covered up in his home studio. The next day he found the death card of the Tarot deck on his night table. At work he took a beast bath as Philamena was off Fridays and this still did not quiet his frightened heart. And the beasts's staring eyes seemed to say, "See, you are the prey, now."

Still he continued his search for Pan and the dyads or water sprites. He saw the dyads first. Two Catholic school girls flounced by his work studio, laughing and punching each other. They were twins, thin and willowy with Titian red hair, just in the first bloom of womanhood. They were cool, ethereal beauties with faces from the past and the long, white alabaster necks and pert, little breasts. He put on his nerd face and asked them if they wanted a tour of his studio which they accepted in a crescendo of laughter. While they wandered about he made his call to Lurch who said he would be right over. He then asked if they'd like to taste some wine. They said he was a dirty old man and he turned into the Boy Scout Master and convinced it was the last thing that was on his mind, and could he sculpt their faces just for fun. They were flattered and quite pleased. When Lurch arrived they became alarmed and said he looked evil. As if on cue, Lurch replied," Er, yes, some find me a tad creepy. I'm as harmless as a cat. a mountain lion," he intoned in his baritone voice and he restrained them as Raz chloroformed them.

They arrived at the studio at the mansion and then Raz had a change of heart. "I can't, Lurch, these are kids: I can't harm them. I know, we'll be exposed. Use your favorite method. Convince them that you'll off their entire family if they tell. Do that thing you do Where you cut open a vein and say, 'This is what I'II do to myself: imagine what I'll do to you.' Tell them you've got their addresses and give them each twenty thousand dollars to hush up. I've got it in the safe and impress on them they can't tell their parents where they got the money."

Thereafter, Raz had the eerie sensation he was being watched at his work. Several times, he almost caught the interloper. So he decided to hide across the street and wait for the mystery guest. It turned out to be Anastasia, one of the twins. When confronted she said she was the evil twin, and wanted to be his apprentice, and not to tell Ondine, the "Good One".

She said she went with old men for the money and that she was a mistress or a dominatrix and never had to actually make love to them: she wanted to be her own woman and not a housewife like her mother. She hated school, knew the career of a dancer was limited so she wanted to be a taxidermist. Raz was intrigued by this chain smoking, gutsy urchin and he took her on. He arranged for her to do general cleaning at first and then to learn taxidermy when Philamena was not there. Anastasia was smitten with Philamena and was not ashamed of her inclinations. Philamena kindly and gracefully refused her advances explaining that she planned to marry Raz. "You're the plus to my negative. Life as algebra," laughed Anastasia who preferred to be called Stash. And it was true. Philamena would say to an ugly girl, "I like your look," while Stash would say, "Oops, better get that hair lip fixed before the wedding…"

Philamena was a hot house orchid while Stash was a nefarious weed.. Raz figured how he could get his dyads from Anastasia and Ondine. He would do a casting of their nude bodies and use his sculptural skill to create the impish faces He would put the sparkle in them: blow life into them. He posed one squatting down with one leg extended cupping a bull frog in her hand: the other was standing platting daises into her long red hair. They were standing ankle deep in a lily pad pond next to a real oak tree. The faces were exquisite, pert and mischievous. Just like they were in real life. The corners of their mouths turned up in merry delight and their wondrous gray eyes sparkled with merriment. By this time Raz had convinced everyone that they were merely sculptures, all of them. Just regular people who posed for him. The girls were nude except for the pubic area where he wove panties of branches, leaves and flowers. At first, Ondine was afraid and timorous but Raz's silly jokes and easy manner won her over. His technique with plastics and polymers was beyond compare. Their "skin" seemed to blush with life and good health. He could create a ruddy complexion as in Bacchus in his 'pards. Everyone was well pleased especially Philamena. She was just so proud of him and excited for his future. Her gentle heart went out to him.

The Job of promotion went out to her as she was "The English Major". Meanwhile, Anastacia and Ondine became a regular fixture around Raz;s studio and Ondine was sweet and endearing as Stash was aggressive and comedic. They took their class mates by on Tuesday for informal gallery parties and one of the students offered to get Raz an appointment with his dad, aa high end advertising executive. At last, the pieces to the puzzle fell into place. Raz's dreams of showing at the Met became all the more real, and closer to fruition.

This is not to say all was well. Raz began to have dreams of the Gypsy dragging him into an open crypt and cannibalizing him or once he lifted Philamena's wedding veil to be affronted by the skeletal head of the Gypsy.

This was not lost on the BFH. "So Erasmus are we afraid of the Gypsy now. Having bad dreams, are we? You're no artiste: you're a pervert and a murderer. How do you think that beautiful girl would react if she knew the truth? Raz, the penultimate artiste! Raz, the philanthropist? You're doomed. Doomed! Doomed. Philamena having sex with someone who slept with his dead mother whom he murdered. EUW! Ill, ill, ill. HAAAA!"

Raz lay on his studio floor and screamed and screamed. Then he called Lurch and said he had to kill and to meet him at the studio. The God Thanatos had Raz in his grasp. They drove to the circus with the idea to get his Pan. And they got him in the personage of the head announcer of the ring. He was like a poster of a fifties horror movie. He had preternaturally bright green eyes with bushy black brows and a gamin, elfish like face with thick red lips and a mouthful of sharp, pointy teeth, the kind of man of whom could be said, the butler did it. He was a dwarf with a barrel chest and short runty legs.

"Sorry, no rubes allowed past this point, mates," he said in a baritone voice.

Lurch smiled his maniacal smile, and said, "Ask not for whom the bell tolls," and grabbed him up and chloroformed him.

Back at the studio, he was begging for his life when he saw all the taxidermied forms.

"You're my last creation," said Raz which did little to calm him.

"I even know where the Leprechauns keep their gold. I'll take you there…." he ventured.

"You get your choice of a last meal. And Leprechauns are fictitious," said Raz.

"Aye, mate, they're not. I'm one of them," said the man.

"And I've got Cinderella turning tricks down at the corner," said Raz. "I'm gonna call you Portnoy because It appears you've got a complaint."

"Name's Sam Picador. Geez, I can easily think of a dozen places where I'd rather be right now."

"Can't we all. Paris on the Seine," said Raz.

"In my own bed with Fat Martha, my wife." said Sam.

Lurch guffawed. He was too inept socially to engage in witty repartee

After a tasty meal of bangers and mash and Guiness Stout. Sam ventured on the meaning of life. Raz said, "That's an easy one. First let me have some crackers and cheese."

"What is it then?" asked Sam.

"Basically, it's winning and losing. One more than the other."

With that utterance, Lurch got up and clouted him on the top of the head killing him instantly. "I can't abide witty conversation," he said matter of factly. "Shall I saw him under the ass?"

"Pour qua non," said Raz who sometimes liked to irritate Lurch.

"I wish you wouldn't go all Maurice Chevalier on me, bitch," he said.

Then they took up the flushing tools and skinned him and destroyed the body waste in a vat of lime. Just a coupla' guys working hard. When it came time to attach the goat hind quarters he used steel reinforcement to strengthen the back legs. He put a leer on his face. He was masterful and proud of his creation.

When he showed it to DOM she said he looked lascivious enough to be Pan and tongue kissed her "handsome son". It should be noted that Raz covered Pan's privates with nettles and wild grasses.

DOM said he looked like a midget named Jack she once fraternized with and let out a raucous laugh saying she was "Balling the Jack."

"So when are we getting together again, sonny boy?" she quipped.

"Never, Mom, I know you're doing Lurch. That should be enough," he replied.

"So what will you do if Philamena finds out the truth behind your creations?"

"I can't think on it without going crazy, Mom. I'd rather be dead than loose her."

"You're really in love, Erasmus. I never thought I'd see the day. No, I won't call you, Raz."

"I'd be a cloud without a sky without her. She is part of my soul and, yes, we make love. I knew that was your next question," he said.

"Beware of the Gypsy. She has something very dark in store for you. She's constantly threatening me," said DOM. "Is she in your dreams?"

"Yes. Last night she tore my heart out from my chest and devoured it right before my eyes. It scares Philamena to see me so afraid. I tell her I can't recall them," he said.

The BFH saw his vulnerability and took this as an opportunity.

"Euw. Ill, Doctor Death regrets. He's terrified and rightly so. We know how it will end. We know! We know! We know!"

Raz became completely unstrung, and decided to go see Philamena to assuage hiss fear and grief. Before going there he decided to go to one of his favorite shops, The Bare Necessities, a lingerie shop, to pick up something for his girl. He saw it right away, a white satin, camisole, an antique, with light blue ribbons interlaced in it. He could ever imagine the platinum haired Philamena in loud raunchy colors like red or hot pink: she was his sodden angel torn from the top of a Christmas tree.

She was delighted, and put it on right away. She was enshrouded in her silver light and glowed like a candle in the dark. He put up her soft, fragrant hair in a truly Victorian bun and told her he was the highwayman come to the old Inn door. She smelled of chamomile and lilacs. She had the pale aspect of a dead person and he was well pleased and grabbed her under the neck to feel life coursing through her veins and thought I could kill her right now and no one would be the wiser. He gently laid her out on her pink satin four poster bed, and felt the lushness of her pomegranate flavored slit engulf him and he took her gentle like the white lily she was yet this was leading to his ferocity when he plundered her like a ten cent dolly. It was a kind of rapture and a great release for both of them. He never asked her if she came. It was an unsaid rule. They lay in each other's arms until the morning etched the walls a soft rose pink. They said not a word for words dilute love. "The Road was a ribbon of moonlight across the purple moor", Alson. Then Philamenai sat bolt upright and said, "I'm famished: last one down's a rotten egg." When he got down Philamena was in her garden picking daisies: she came in flushed from the wind and threw the daises on the table and began cutting them down to put in a glass crystal vase on the breakfast table. She whirled around the kitchen like a dervish, making coffee, cracking eggs, cutting up vegetables, and whipping a batch of blueberry pancakes. He was well pleased and like all thin girls she ate like a horse.

He took her hands in his and said, "Phil if you were to find out something unsavory about me would you still love me?

"Just tell me what. Insanity in the family, dead bodies in a trunk, what," she asked.

"Not exactly, but close. There are parts of me you don't know, darling." he said.

"Is that all, silly. We can't ever know each other completely. Do I need a psychiatric syllabus, dear," she quipped. "Perish the thought "You are so easy to love, doll," he murmured.

She jumped in his arms, straddling him with her legs.

Later that day he had his comuppence. His failed Renoir, "Lady with a Red Hat" recognized him on a crowded street and chased him with a pen knife yelling, "I'm gonna, kill you, bastard. Stop that man he is a serial killer." Fortunately people did not want to get involved with a fat lady welding a pen knife and a piece of butter cake. He caught a cab pronto saying 'pissed off ex-wife, got behind in alimony."

The cab driver winked and said, ''Ya sure like 'em with a lot of meat on their bones, like an over ripe peach."

He gave the required chuckle and stilled the rumbling of his heart. He told DOM about it and she had a laugh riot. "I can just see it now. You running like a scalded pup and all that fat jiggling! You know they'll catch you eventually. Crime does not pay."

Chapter Thirteen

C rime does pay, au contraire, mon mere."

"Oh, yeah, like you're going to get that gig at the Met…" said DOM.

"You're wrong, Mommy, crime pays very well. I'm scheduled for April, The Cruelist Month. The same month as the wedding and you may just get those grandchildren."

"As I live and die! Really?" she exclaimed.

"Yes, really. We go at it like jack rabbits. She likes my dick. Never mind where it's been. Mommy you and Philamena should know I've made provision for you in my will. There's a trust for each of you and Esmeralda, your caretaker is also covered."

"I won't need it, sonny boy, I shall opt to be really dead, door nail dead if anything happens to you, Erasmus," said DOM.

"Oh, yeah, you say that now. Like do you really think you'll end up heaven. Here's the name of the lawyer, Stutz Grimlicker: I got him from Lurch. And I also hired an accountant to rein in the lawyer if necessary. Checks and balances, you know. When there's a lot of money involved honest people become crooks. The Root of all Evil, etc."

"Just how much are we talking about, doll?" asked DOM.

"You're a gruesome old doll to ask," said Raz.

"Oh, like I'd off you for it."

"The thought may have crossed my mind," admitted Raz. "And you're still balling Lurch and he'd kill for a nickel. He's in my will, too. He'll be able to buy all the tail west of Tia Juana."

"Can't even trust his own mother," she sniffed.

"That's a given. Love you, Mom," he said.

"Love you, too, son. Give Mommy a smoochie."

And her eye fell out and rolled under the bed. Like any good son he retrieved it. "There, all beautiful again," he said.

"That's a given," said DOM.

Then Raz went to have a talk with Philamena regarding his imminent demise. The BFH took it as an opportunity to devil him. "Oh, Boo Hoo, the Gypsy's going to do him in. He's scared shitless. It's gonna' be a long, painful death: rest assured. Oh, poor Erasmus. Boo Hoo Hoo."

Philamena noticed he looked ill and that he broke out in a cold sweat and did her best to soothe him. By this token she took him to bed. The pink satin sheets looked like an open vagina. She slipped into her Black Orchid outfit: this was the other side of the coin, the dark side of the moon. She put on a black leather bustier with lacy thong undies and thigh high black patent leather boots and brandished a cat o' nine tails. She sat on the edge of the bed and told him to strip down and crawl towards her. When he got close she lashed him twice across the shoulders with a cat of nine tails and she pulled her panties to the side and said, "Eat me like the fucking slave you are, Daddy." She smelled like a rotten nectarine. She forced his head down so hard she could barely breathe: half an hour later she arched back and screamed. It was not a human scream. Then she bound and blind folded him and rode him like succubus. He was overcome with raw lust. In the end she forced him to eat raw meat and then released him into a splendorous heaven. He slept like a soul damned to hell.

He awoke to the late afternoon sun slanting into the room and Philamena was massaging ointment into his wounds. She had on one of her midi tee shirts (pale yellow) and a pair of lace undies (baby blue). Her hair was in pigtails and she sported Mickey Mouse ears on her head. She had her poetry manuscripts spread out on the bed, open in hand.

"First the drama: now the comedy," she said and laughed.

"Mind telling me who I was sleeping with this afternoon?" he said.

"Oh, her, that's The Black Orchid: I guess she came to me when I was about eight. I used to murder my dolls. Smash their heads. hang them, burn them, and I used to slip laxatives into daddy's beer when he wasn't looking. I was me, little, scared Philamena and then she was just there one day and I began to laugh every time he abused me and oft times I was the aggressor. Boy was he surprised. He never knew what hit him. I began to give him orders, and he liked it. When I was The Black Orchid I wasn't afraid and I didn't feel afraid. She keeps me safe.

"They used to call that multiple personality disorder: the call it dissociative disorder, now, Philamena," said Raz.

"Schlemeil, I don't ever want to hear that shit coming out of your mouth, and she punched him in the gut. "I know myself very well. Don't make a graft of me. Don't study me like some insect or cell culture. II don't pry into your secrets do I?"

"Well, hot damn, we have our little hissy fit, don't we? I'm gonna' tickle you until you bust a gut."

"You wouldn't dare," she hissed.

"I would dare," he said and proceed to rough her up, alternately spanking her and tickling her. She had a spasm of laughing as did he.

Afterward, they decided to go a fancy restaurant and behave real haut. He wore an Armani tux and she wore a white Halston sheath with silver threads running through it and high green Chartreuse shoes and emerald dangling ear rings. He ordered for the both of them, Esargot, Coq Au Vin, asparagus spears, tomato aspic summer squash, and a fruit medley of raspberries green grapes and bananas. They ordered five French desserts. For aperitifs they ordered Sambucca.

"Well, this is as good a time as any to break the news to your Raz, I'm pregnant," said Philamena.

Raz turned bright red and sputtered, "Pregnant...it's wonderful, Phil. Listen people" he said to the house, "drinks for everyone. My girl is pregnant."

"Do I hear wedding bells?" said a nearby matron.

Raz replied. "This April in two months. April is the Cruelest Month. T.S. Eliot..."

Then he heard raucous laughter from the BFH.

When they got back to Raz's mansion Raz decided he had better have a talk with Philamena. It was about her future and of course, his imminent demise.

"Darling, I think I better apprise you of the situation. I screwed with the wrong people once and I think they may come after me. It's really bad. Now, hush I can't tell you who.. In the event of my death you will be well protected financially. I was raised without a father, so I kinda' came into my manhood late. Like at thirty. When all options run out one becomes a man. The main thing is a man has to do gainful work. That's the main thing; secondly, a man must show mercy to weaker beings. Everybody should have ambition like you with your poetry. Raise our children to want something from life. Raise them to love themselves. You're so gentle, Phil, I cannot see how you can go wrong.

As for other men. Watch out for fortune hunters: and make sure they'll be good fathers. The world is full of men who would love you: you're a beauty inside and out. I want you to be with someone though to hurts me to say it. It hurts so bad. But life goes on, Phil. Now stop crying, honey. "Going to the chapel and we're gonna' get married", as the song goes. I'll be late as I have work to do at the shop. Don't wait up for me."

But, it was not to the shop he went. He went trolling for whores, the nastiest, most raunchy, debauched ones. The idea of Philamena with other hands on her was driving him mad. He got the oldest, most defunct, toothless one he could find. He ended her life in one fell swoop and came massively. After all, Raz was a killer.

Chapter Fourteen

Raz took old Cindy Lou, as he called her to a sheet metal dump and put her body in the trunk. It would be like an ice cream sandwich once she got crushed with her as the ice cream he thought. He picked one flower weed up and placed it on the trunk. No funeral is complete without flowers.

When he got back, he found Philamena in tears. A lot had happened while he was gone. The early morning sun cast an eerie, garish aspect to the house kindo like a crime scene. It seems that Philamena told the children of her impending pregnancy and Emile went ballistic grabbing a hammer and smashing all his sister's dolls: then he went catatonic slumped into a corner.

"I don't know what happened. He was fine one moment: then suddenly he went berserk. I tried to talk to him, hold him but he's so stiff. And Suzie's so upset and doesn't know what's wrong with her brother. It's like his soul fled his body," she said.

Raz took Philamena in his arms and brought Suzie over for a group hug. "Poor little bugger. He thought that we would abandon him now that we have a biological child. Get on the phone to his therapist, Phil. He'll have to be hospitalized. He'll have to stay there for a while. We'll just have to give him extra love and reassurance when he gets out," said Raz. And all went well just like in the movies. Best of all possible Worlds.

Meanwhile, Raz had to prepare for his upcoming wedding and the show at The Met. He was billed as "America's Premier Sculptor" and a large picture of his Botticelli's Venus on the Half Shell was used in the print and television ads. Reporters were always accosting him, trying to get a scoop on him. He drew an emphatic view of himself. Poor boy with disadvantaged background, sole caretaker of disabled mother until she died when he was totally bereft. Great success as taxidermist lead to experimenting with clay sculpturing. The rest is history. So to speak. It all started with his bird collection. Taxidermy.

Raz knew how to put a spin on any story. Massive amounts of invitations to his opening were sent out to his friends, and prominent art collectors, media mavens and fashion magazines in which ads were placed.

On the day of the reception, Raz was as nervous as a Thunder bolt. Two cats fighting it out in a burlap bag couldn't have been more nervous. He had on his Armani suit and was pacing back and forth. Philamena, cool as a summer breeze, brought in a chilled bottle of champagne, and enshrouded him in her calmness. There is great power in silence. She was dressed in a pink linen sheath with high, chartreuse pumps and a silver clasp purse. She had pink roses intertwined in her silver hair and wore dangling emerald ear rings and an emerald choker.

The patrons were like a crowd scene from a Hercules movie with much "oohing and awing". The rustling of the satin and brocade materials of the ladies' gowns and the ethereal scents of their perfumes soothed Raz's jangled nerves like water over a hot stone. The greeter was an Alfred Hitchcock look alike with a British accent and Raz was well pleased. The works were shown in the marigold colored room with the balconies. The children were not present as their dead parents were part of the exhibit. The mother was a Degas dancer in green gauze tutu and pink toe shoes and she was lit by an eerie green light from underneath which played on her deathly pale skin. The father was Bacchus, the Greek God of Drink with his two 'pards (leopards) He wore a bear skin loincloth, and his husky, boisterous body was well displayed. His face was bawdy and roguish and mischievous. He held up an iron tankard of red wine jovially as if to invite all to join him.

Botticelli's Venus on the Half Shell was the stand out of the show. Her Renaissance face was perfect in all detail including her beautiful grey blue eyes. Her skin gave of a kind of pinkish light as if she were vibrantly alive. People could not resist touching her and found her oddly human feeling. Raz tossed it off to his secret brand of polymers and plastics. Her pert breasts stood out like two hard nectarines and her body was long, full and languorous, and her sex like the painting, was obscured by a lock of her hair.

The twins frolicking as water sprites in a small lily pad pond were the only true statues in the show The rest had once been human. Yahweh, a huge man stood in wrathful silence clutching three stylized thunderbolts in his left hand and a raised cane in his right as if to strike someone down. His face was perilous to look on so wrathful it was. He wore a sackcloth monk's robe which did not obscure the massiveness of his body. His burnt sienna eyes conveyed such rage and malice they were mesmerizing. It was like falling into a vat of acid.

In stark contrast to Yahweh, Raz'z god, Pan, radiated merriment and good will and the goat legs were well fitted to his somewhat paunchy torso. He grinned impishly and his green eyes seemed to actually look back at the people. He was playing the flute. The sound of the medieval music was piped in and had an eerie quality, His genital region was festooned with branches, nettles and leaves. He had the looks of a prankster, or a card cheat.

The patrons surrounded Raz with all sorts of questions about his source of inspiration for these creations and he drolly said, "The People on the street." He also confessed to being self taught in art and literature, particularly mythology. To a patron, an artist is just another curio, a walnut to crack wide open, and of course, creative, but a lessor person. Heaven Knows Wealth Rules The World. Some of the rich women wanted to go slumming with the "Artiste" and gave him their cards and in one case a pair of black lace panties with her malodorous scent on them. It smelled like a cat box. This was done when Philamena was riveting the patrons with tales of Raz's funny exploits which never happened and tales of his warm and happy childhood. No one is interested in damaged people and Philamena relied on the old television reruns of "Father Knows Best" where every cloud has a silver lining and all problems can be solved. People don't like heartache: They think it's contagious.

Raz liked the old cougar who gave him her panties and tongued him in the ear. He liked outrageous people and FiFi LeFarge was certainly that. Model thin and dangerously glamorous with her ermine wrap and drenched in diamonds

Her skin resembled a dried river bed. But, Ah! The beautiful features and the scent of lavender trailing behind her and the bold saunter. A keeper! He sent her one dozen yellow roses and a box of

Godiva chocolates the next day. A friend indeed but alas, not a lover. He was certain he could win her over.

They left the Met considerably richer than they went in. God loves a rich man just as much as a poor man. Contrary to Popular Mythology,

Chapter Fifteen

On April 14, Raz and Philamena went to city hall to get married and Raz thought "Geez, these people in here shouldn't get married much less leave their houses. Their progeny would surely look like the baby out of EraserHead."

They skipped to Raz's red Lamborghini like two kid and felt giddy with anticipation. And the first thing that came on the car radio was "Another one bites the dust." They had a laugh riot, The second song was Etta James's "At Last." "At last my love has come along/ my lonely days are over and my life is like a song."

"Raz, do you think love has a shelf life?"

"Let's have a very civil divorce. I'll give you the house, lots of moola and joint custody of the kids. You see, I'll always take care of you Philamena even to the grave. And no damn pre-nup as my lawyer keeps pushing."

"I love you, Razberry. So much," said Philamena. "If we divorce let's hit it once in a while,"

"That's a given, Hon."

She asked Raz who he invited to the wedding saying she only invited her nine brothers, no mother or dad.

"Let's see close personal friends, Mamie June and her eighty kids. There will be pony rides and games. Should be fun for Suzie and Emile. My Latina friends, Lula and Salameh, my boss, Don Udon and family. Otherwise total strangers. Patrons, media people, fashion people, weight lifters, stand-up comics and Le Cirque Soleil. I want it to be like a Fellini movie and it will all be outside in back of the Estate on the lawn. Got one five hundred seats and tables. By the way, I've made Lurch the Greeter to take coats and give out place cards to inject a little "noiir" into the proceedings. Listen, at the opening, some of the fashion people evinced an interest in you. Take all you can get in this life, Philamena. 'Ere time's winged is drawing near'. I don't want you stuck in some musty taxidermy shop all your life. Share your beauty with the world."

Are you crazy, Raz?"

"Yes, isn't it wonderful, Philamena?"

"Rather, so," she replied. "What are we serving?

"A full liquor cabinet, lobster and steak and chicken. Green beans almondine, garlic mash potatoes, squashes sautéed in olive oil, grain breads, candied yams, ad infinitum. There will be a cheese table and a desert table of French pastries. Then coffee and desert liquers. I love a party: we never had them when I was a kid. Listen to me. If something should happen to me, carry on. Have the damn party. Swear to it, Philamena."

"I swear, Razberry but what on earth could go wrong."

"I don't know but I have done some very bad things and it might just catch up with me," said Raz. "Sometimes great beauty can come from an ugly place."

The wedding was beautiful with people fanning themselves in anticipation. All heads were turned to see Suzie as flower girl sprinkling rose petals in the aisle as the music cued up, and the groom flanked by Salameh and Lula took his place at the altar. Philamena delivered by her red headed, six foot four brother could've made an angel look like a slut. She glowed with her silver light and smelled of gardenias. Her azure eyes moist with tears were like stars in a night sky.

The preacher droned on in a monotone and Raz heard the BFH screaming "You're gonna' get yours now, Boy Scout" Raz began to feel stiff all over and Ill. He put the ring on her and lifted the veil to kiss her. He could not feel the softness of her lips. When he tried to get down from the podium he could not move. He was taxidermy and he saw the gypsy's mirthful eyes for a moment.

Philamena kept saying "I know he's alive in there somewhere. I can feel him. He's Marilyn Monroe dead" She squelched a racking sob and said, "Continue the party. It is what he would have wanted. With her finger tips she wiped some viscous matter from under his eyes. It might have been tears.

Printed in the United States
By Bookmasters